NAKED INNOCENCE

The Bastille Day Murder

A Tony Felice, PI, Mystery

Geno Azevedo

NAKED INNOCENCE
The Bastille Day Murder

A Tony Felice, PI, Mystery
www.TonyFeliceMystery.com

Design and layout by Mark E. Anderson
www.AquaZebra.com

Cover illlulstration by Troy K. Caperton
www.troycap.com

Print on Demand by Lightning Source
A division of Ingram Books

Azevedo Publishing Company
Palm Springs, CA

Because of the dynamic nature of the Internet, any web addresses or links contained in this book may have changed since publication and may no longer be valid.

ISBN: 978-1-4276-4973-7

ISBN lists Aardvark Global Publishing as the publisher

Library of Congress Control Number: 2011911705

Printed in the United States of America

First Edition
First Printing, July 2011

Dedication

This book is dedicated
to my long-time dear friend, Kay.
Kay was instrumental in the
development of my sexuality.
She is a very special person in my life
and I am eternally grateful to her.

This one's for you Kay—Thanks.

Disclaimer

This book is a work of fiction. The characters, incidents, and dialogue are drawn from the author's imagination and are not to be construed as real. Any resemblance to actual events or persons, living or dead, is entirely coincidental.

About the Author

Geno is no stranger to the naturist community and he has chosen to share his life experiences vicariously with you thru the character of Antonio Vito Felice, PI. This is the second book in the series, the first being NAKED DICK.

He is a native Californian who worked for many years in Public Service employment before his retirement to Palm Springs. The desert sun provides ample opportunity to enjoy life with little or no textile confinement and writing is a good pastime.

Watch for more Tony Felice, PI mystery books to follow. You'll get caught up in his adventurous life and eagerly anticipate the release of book three in the series coming soon.

Contents

NAKED INNOCENCE

The Bastille Day Murder

A Tony Felice, PI, Mystery

Geno Azevedo

Preface

The Bastille Day Murder

"Tony, I'm glad I caught you. I'm afraid I have some bad news. Your good friend was murdered Saturday night."

I could feel the blood drain from my head and I felt faint. I was sick to my stomach to think that someone would deliberately kill this sweet innocent man.

"Sorry to be the one to break the news to you, but better that you should hear it from me than to read it in the paper."

I had solved my first big murder case last year in northern California and felt good about my skills as a Private Investigator. I never dreamed the next big case for me would be investigating the death of my dear friend.

1

Returning Home

"Ladies and Gentlemen, this is your captain speaking. We'll soon be on the ground at San Diego Airport where the temperature currently is a comfortable 88 degrees. Please be sure your seatbelt is fastened, and remain in your seat until we have come to a full stop at the airport terminal. Thank you."

As the plane's tires screeched at contact with the tarmac, I couldn't avoid the smile that came to my face. It was good to be home again, but my week undercover investigating a suspected murder in northern California was hardly like work. I'd solved my first big case, the killer was arrested, and I'd forged some amazing new friendships in the gay nudist community.

It had been quite a stretch for me to go undercover in a nudist resort in order to investigate this case. Along the way, however, I learned something about myself. For years I'd felt uncomfortable with my body and would blush at the sight of my naked image in the mirror stepping out of the shower. I think this came from the idea I had, like many people have, that nudity equates to sex. And sex to me is a private and personal expression.

After being around this group of naturists for a week, I realized that nudity is not a sexual thing unless you want it to be. All of these guys were so comfortable in their own skin that they literally had nothing to hide. I learned to see the person inside and not the clothing on the outside. After all, we come into this world naked as a baby, and we learn that society now dictates clothes to be necessary in social settings. So, nudity of itself, I discovered, is very natural. And to my surprise, I really enjoyed my week at Rancho Sierra, and hoped I could remain in touch with some of the new friends I had made at this beautiful Cosumnes River resort.

It was late Sunday afternoon when my plane landed in San Diego and I was glad I'd planned to take the next day off to get adjusted to the idea of going back to work. My office is not one of high stress unless I'm working on an intense case, but I felt sure there would be a lot of paperwork to sort through. We handle a variety of cases ranging from divorce to murder. My boss, Vince Castillo, is a very easy going kinda guy. He owns Balboa Private Investigators, but being in his seventies he is not long before retirement. Since he has no heirs interested in the business, I hope someday to be able to buy him out. Until that time, I'm learning as much about the business from him that I can.

I'm only 34, so I have a lot to learn. I've thoroughly enjoyed the last four years working as a private dick for Vinnie, but I do have a social life here San Diego as well. Living in the Hillcrest is so convenient to the gay night life. I live alone in my small condo and I like it that way. I'm sort of a neat freak, so it would be difficult to adjust to a roommate, let alone a husband.

"Here we are." I had dozed off during the cab ride home from the airport. Guess I was more tired out from the week than I'd realized. I had plenty to do that evening and the next day, but not a lot of dirty laundry after a nudist vacation. I had other errands to run to get ready for work. It was nice to be home.

I was looking forward to calling Brad too. Bradley Fisher, a former boyfriend of mine who had dumped me and hurt me badly, had recently called and indicated he would like to get together for dinner. I was very skeptical, not wanting to be hurt again, but I still had a love for Brad that I couldn't deny. As with a school girl crush, I got butterflies at the thought of calling him. What if he gives me the "let's just be friends" line … or what if he'd changed his mind about getting together? From the message he left on my cell phone he sounded excited to get together, but I still worried that maybe I was reading too much into it.

Brad and I had dated for nearly a year, and just when

I thought things were going well with us, he decided he was "bored" with our relationship, and wanted to break it off. What is that supposed to mean ... "bored?" At that time I was in denial, and thought it was something we could work through. When it really hit home with me was when he showed up at a friend's party with a date. That caught me off guard and really hurt me, and I vowed never to let him or any other man hurt me like that ever again.

Yet, here I was scheming to go out with Brad again, in hopes that maybe this time would be different. If it was my life that Brad felt was boring back then, that was certainly not the case any longer. My life was far from boring now. On the other hand, maybe I might be the one needing to step back from the possibility of a relationship with Brad. I might find myself over this crush after spending time with Brad once again. We had both grown up and changed since our little tryst and the compatibility might not be there.

Tuesday morning, I was up early and ready for work. I felt good about myself, having solved my first really big investigation case. I hoped that my boss, Vinnie, would be impressed enough to give me a raise and some sort of recognition but that was doubtful. I poured myself one last cup of coffee in my traveler mug and took the elevator to the basement garage to my car. I felt confidence in my stride as I walked through the front door of my office.

"Good morning Ton ... y, err ... Mr. Felice, and welcome back!"

'Mr. Felice?' ... Jenn hadn't called me that since the first week I started work here. I guess my accomplishments solving this murder had earned me a newfound respect from the office staff. But I found the formality uncomfortable. "Thank you, Jenn ... uh Jennifer. It's good to be back."

Jennifer Rogers was the receptionist when I started working at Balboa Investigators. I'm not sure how many years she's been working there, but it must be ten or more. She is good at what she does, but then each investigator keeps track of his own case load and works up his own notes. Jenn pretty much acts only as a receptionist, and I get along well with her. I think she likes gay boys ... we can relate.

"Mr. Felice, Mr. Castillo would like to see you in his office as soon as you get settled in this morning. ... There's a fresh pot of coffee I just made. Can I get you a cup?"

"Thanks, Jenn, but I can get my own. ... Oh, and Jenn ..."

"Yes, Mr. Felice?"

"Please, just call me Tony, like before, and if you don't mind, I'll still call you Jenn."

"That sounds perfect, Mr. ... Tony. Oh and by the way, you had a call this morning from a gentleman who said to tell you Patrick called and for you to call him when you get in. He didn't leave his number ... said you would know how to reach him."

"Thanks, Jenn. Yes, Patrick's a friend of mine. I'll call him later."

I poured myself a cup of coffee in the break room and then returned to my office to try and make some sense of the pile of correspondence waiting for me. My office is small but provides the privacy needed to discuss with clients the personal problems with which they are seeking help. Each of Vinnie's investigators has his own office and although there are no windows in each office, there is a row of fixed glass panes just below the ceiling level to provide natural lighting. It's not a bad space at all and much of my work is done out in the field or at home so I don't spend a lot of time in my office ordinarily.

Why is it when you leave town for a week you have to work twice as hard to get caught up when you get back? Before I got too involved with this mess, I knew I'd better get in to see my boss.

Knock, knock! "Good morning, Vinnie!"

"Hey ... there he is ... my star investigator! Welcome back, Tony!"

Let's see if 'star investigator' will translate into dollar signs. "Good to be back, Vinnie!"

"Tony, I'm so happy with you right now with the job you did up north that I could kiss you … but then the rest of my staff might get the wrong idea." <Chuckle, chuckle!>

"Thanks, Vinnie!"

"All the reports from the Rancho Sierra resort, and from the Sheriff's Department, have been nothing but complimentary toward you. You conducted yourself as a true professional."

"Well, this was certainly a big opportunity for me, Vinnie … and I appreciate the confidence you had in assigning me to this investigation." Of course, the fact that I'm the only gay man Vinnie has on his staff may have contributed to that confidence too, since this was an assignment at a gay resort. The nudity thing had caught me by surprise, though.

"To show my appreciation, Tony, I'm promoting you to 'Senior Private Investigator.'"

"Wow, thanks, Vinnie."

"I think you probably know, Tony, there's a five percent pay differential between your current position and this new title?"

"I didn't realize it's that much of an increase. That's great and it'll sure come in handy. Thanks again, Vinnie."

"Thank YOU, Tony, for your commitment to me and this firm. I'll let Jennifer know to have new business cards printed up for you, and your next paycheck should reflect the salary increase."

"I really appreciate it."

"Oh … and you'll notice a few new investigation cases I left on your desk for you. Nothing too exciting yet, but when I do get a big case for you, I'll surely send it your way."

"Thanks again, Vinnie. Guess I'd better get at it."

I was actually surprised that Vinnie was so anxious to recognize my accomplishments. Even though I was pleased with my performance, I expected I might have to pat myself on the back and toot my own horn, but that was not the case.

Returning to my office I decided I'd better return my bff Patrick's call since he'd missed me earlier in the morning. I was anxious to hear about the Palm Springs White Party. I had planned to join him and some other friends for the event before getting assigned to this case in northern California. I'm sure from some of the rumors about the week, it had been very entertaining to say the least and I was sorry to have missed out. However, my trip up north was quite the experience too and I would not have wanted to miss it … even for the White Party.

I was excited to tell Patrick all about my trip too. Although we're best friends, it's not all that often we get together since he and his partner Frank live in WeHo and I'm of course here in the Hillcrest area of San Diego and rarely get to West Hollywood. I was hoping we could try to get together again soon.

I had met Patrick about eight years ago during Gay

Night at Disneyland. We were waiting in line to ride Pirates of the Caribbean and I found him attractive and struck up a conversation. I had gone to the event alone and soon hooked up with Patrick and his friends to spend a crazy evening together. The friendship continued and it has only grown stronger over the years, but never a romantic relationship between us. Patrick was already dating Frank at the time.

As his phone rang, I shuffled some of the papers on my desk with a sigh of frustration at the pile. "Hey, Tony, how are you?" His iPhone had identified me calling.

"Good, Patrick. It's good to be back."

"I'll bet ... and actually, I'm glad to be back from Palm Springs too. Not sure I could take another day of partying. ... Gettin' too old for that, Tony!"

"Hey, I hear you, Patrick. But did you have a good time? That's all that matters. I want to hear all about it."

"It was great, Tony. The Lady Gaga performance was awesome. You would have loved it ... I want to hear all about your nudie adventure in Sacramento."

"Yeah, I've got a lot to tell you."

"Well, Tony ... Frank has a gig in San Diego toward the end of this week and the company is putting him up at the Four Seasons."

"Wow, how nice!"

"Yeah, that's what I thought. So the little 'wife' is going to join him overnight for a little pampering at the spa and poolside. Can you join me for a day of fun?"

"Oh my gawd, as nice as that sounds, I really can't take any more time away from my office right now. You would not believe the pile on my desk that I'm looking at."

"Damn … I was afraid you might say that. Guess I'll have to go it alone. Are you free to get together for dinner Thursday evening?"

"That should work. It would be great to see you and Frank and hear all about the White Party."

"Yeah, and as I said, I want to hear of your adventures too. So let's plan on dinner Thursday at 7:00 … no, better make it 7:30 … I'm not sure when Frank will be done with work that evening."

"Sounds great, Patrick!"

"I'll make reservations for us at Martini Above Fourth and we'll meet you there."

"Great. Thanks, Patrick. See you Thursday evening."

"See you there."

As we hung up, my thoughts drifted to how fortunate I am to have friends like Patrick—and I hoped that some of my new naturist friends would become close friends too. And then … almost like some sort of mental telepathy, my iPhone rang. I knew from the area code it was not a local call. With an area code of 503, who could this, be? … Probably a sales call.

"Hello?"

"Hey, is this my naked bud?"

I could recognize that deep sexy voice anywhere. It was Eric whom I'd met up at Rancho Sierra, one of my newfound naturist buddies. "Hey Eric, I was just thinking of you and some of my other buds from last week. How did you get my phone number?"

"Cris and Mike gave it to me. I guess you guys exchanged numbers before leaving the resort."

"Wow, what a pleasant surprise. Good to hear from you."

"Well, I didn't get much of a chance to say goodbye when you left Sunday, so I thought I'd call you. I just wanted to let you know I want to keep in touch and make sure you have my number."

"Great, I do now and will add you to my list of contacts. I really enjoyed meeting you and many of the other guys."

"Kewl ... I'm glad you warmed up to the idea of a bunch of naked men in the woods." <Ha, ha!>

"Oh yeah!"

"Well ... look, bud, I know you're probably at work and I don't want to keep you, but I wanted to check in with you and let you know we need to keep in touch. You should come up to Portland some time and see us. It's not all that warm up this way, but we can run around the house naked and 'H' can just look the other way."

"That's right ... you did tell me your partner 'H' is not into the nudity thing. Is that a problem in your relationship?"

"Not really, Tony. He does his thing and I do mine

and then we still do things together whenever we can. I'm very fortunate to have such an understanding husband who realizes the nudity vacations are not about sex."

"I'm starting to realize that now."

"So, think about coming up to visit soon."

"Sounds like a plan. Maybe if I come during the summer you can take me to that beach you talked about?"

"Rooster Rock? You got yourself a deal. Let's plan on it."

"Great! ... Well, thanks for calling, Eric, and hope to see you or talk to you soon."

"Sure thing. Later, Dude!"

What a pleasant surprise that was, and here I was just wondering if I'd ever hear from any of those guys again. I made a lot of great friendships over that week with some really awesome guys. With Cris and Michael, I'd felt an almost instant bond. They live in Sacramento and have been together for many years. Eric was another guest that week with whom I formed a bond very quickly. Everyone I met that week impressed me as being very genuine and sincere.

Well, enough for wasting away the day dreaming. I knew I'd better get down to business and quit putting off the inevitable of sorting through the pile on my desk, but there was one more call I needed to make before getting back into the routine. I needed to call Brad and let him know I was back in town as I promised him I would.

I could feel the nervous knot developing in the pit of my stomach at the thought of calling him. I'd never really stopped loving this man, even though I tried to convince my friends that it was over and I was done with him. Maybe this time, things would be different ... *'maybe this time he'll stay.'* Was I just fooling myself? I knew I had to give it a shot and see.

His phone was ringing now. ... Oh my gawd, what was I gonna say to him?

"Hello?"

For a split second, I thought about hanging up but I knew I couldn't. I was struck with a deep desire to hear his voice mixed with the sudden realization that he had caller ID. "Hey, Brad, it's Tony."

"I thought I recognized that phone number. How you doing? I take it you're home now?"

Whew ... so glad I didn't hang up. How embarrassing would that have been? "Yeah, I'm home now and it's nice to be back."

"I'll bet. Now ... I think you said you'd been in Sacramento on assignment, is that right?"

"Yeah, it's a long story. I'll have to tell you all about it when you have some time." I chuckled at the thought of me telling him about my nude adventure with 40 other naked men!

"Great, I would love to hear about it. So when can we get together and maybe grab a bite to eat?"

"Well, Brad, what about this weekend?"

"Oh, that's not good for me. ... This weekend I'm

going to Phoenix to visit my Dad."

"Oh, how is he doing?"

"He's hanging in there. Since Mom died it's been rough on him but he's doing well for his age. I'd love to see you before I leave, Tony. Any chance of dinner Thursday night?"

My mind raced with thoughts of my dinner plans with Patrick and what to do. Should I cancel on Patrick? ... Should I invite Brad to join us even though I know Patrick does not care for Brad? ... Should I tell Brad Thursday is not good for me and run the risk of us never reconnecting again? Shit! What to do.

"Well, Brad, would you like to join me as my date for dinner with Patrick and Frank at Martini Above Fourth?"

"Ouch ... damn ... high class! I thought maybe we'd do a simple dinner out, but let's dine in style. Do you think Patrick will allow me to sit at the same table with him and Frank?"

"I'm buying dinner, and don't worry about Patrick. He can just suck it up and act like a big boy for the evening. I would love to have you as my date."

"Well then, it's settled and I look forward to it and to seeing you."

"Great. You can buy me an after-dinner drink."

"So you want me to come by your place and we can walk to the restaurant?"

"Sure. You still know how to get there?"

"Duh ... it wasn't that long ago. What time should I come by?"

"Dinner reservations are for 7:30, so why don't you plan on getting to my place at 6:30 and we can have a glass of wine before we head out to the restaurant?"

"Great. Thanks, Tony. I'll see you Thursday evening."

"Thanks, Brad. I'm looking forward to it ... bye."

Whew, that went rather well after all. Not sure what Patrick was going to do when Brad showed up with me at dinner. I thought about calling him to give him a heads up, but I decided it might be best if I just surprised him. I know how much he loves surprises ... NOT!

Right then I needed to get busy. It was almost noon on my first day back and I hadn't done a damn thing except receive a promotion. Now I guess I'd better earn it.

Buzz ... buzz! My phone signaled me. "Yes, Jenn?"

"Oh ... hi, Tony. Mr. Castillo would like to see you in the reception room."

"Thanks, Jenn."

Now what? Seemed like this was going to be one of those days when nothing would get accomplished. And what was with this meeting Vinnie in the conference room? I stepped out from my office and ... "Surprise!"

The entire office staff, all six investigators, plus one aid and Jenn and Vinnie, were gathered around several large pizza boxes on a table and a *'Congratulations'* banner had been hung on the wall above the table. I think my face went three shades of red with embarrassment.

Vinnie gave a glowing speech to everyone announcing my promotion and commending me on the job I'd done on the murder investigation in northern California. Then he said, ". . . now let's everyone eat some pizza and . . . GET BACK TO WORK!"

2

Courtship

The next couple of days seemed like a blur at work and before I knew it, it was Thursday. All day I spent worrying about seeing Brad that night ... wondering how the evening would be, going out with him again. I had never really gotten over him after he hurt me and walked out of my life, and I didn't want to appear desperate this time. But I wanted to give us a second chance in case he'd changed and was ready for a committed relationship.

When Brad and I were together he made me feel so safe yet so sexual. Just having him next to me he was like my security blanket, and friends told me I would glow with affection for this man when we were together in public. The sexual energy between us was hot and passionate, our bodies fit perfectly together. I never had a sexual partner that I felt so passionate with, so free to express my sexuality and explore each other so freely. Even the times when we just lay in bed cuddling were erotic for me. Just to be able to wake up next to him was all I needed.

Oh geeze! ... What if Brad wanted to stay the night at my place instead of driving home after dinner? As much as I might enjoy that, I really wanted to take things slow this time and make sure I didn't get hurt again. I didn't think Brad would assume he could do that. Would he?

It was now five o'clock and I had left work a little early to straighten up the house and get ready for my big dinner date. I always keep my place presentable but still I stressed out at making sure everything was perfect. My taste in furnishings leans toward modern with simple clean lines. The cool blue-gray walls complement nicely the brushed chrome and leather living room set, and the blond hardwood flooring. I've never been one for a lot of tchotchkes in my decor, but a few appropriately placed accent candles made for an inviting and romantic evening setting. I had purchased some calla lilies that I felt would complete this decor, a setting suitable for *Architectural Digest*.

The thought of what Patrick might do when seeing Brad and me together again made me nervous as well. I decided to open a bottle of wine to help calm my nerves while I waited for Brad's arrival.

The clock read 6:37, I'd had two glasses of wine, and Brad was late. Not a great way to start out the date. Then my phone rang and I could see before answering it that it was Brad calling. My heart skipped a beat. ... Was he calling to cancel?

"Hey, Brad!"

"Hi, Tony. I'm downstairs in the lobby. What is your unit number again?"

"Number 516. When you get off the elevator, head straight down the hall. I'm on the right toward the end."

"Thought so, thanks. I'll be right there."

"Great . . . see you in a bit."

After hanging up the phone, I poured myself a little more wine and decided to step out the door into the hall to catch Brad's attention as he stepped off the elevator.

Ding! The elevator signaled a stop on my floor and as the doors opened, an Adonis was revealed. I felt like my whole world was suddenly moving in slow motion as Brad walked toward me. My heart pounded as if it would leap right from my chest. It was like being in a Calvin Kline commercial as he came closer.

I'd always loved the way Brad looked in his clothes . . . and out of them for that matter. Tonight was no exception. He looked HOT in his Dolce & Gabbana black v-neck cashmere pullover with just enough of his sexy hairy chest showing to give him that masculine, rugged appearance. He wore his sleeves pushed up, exposing his hairy forearms and the bold Movado watch on his wrist, a combination that drove me crazy. I've always been aroused by a man's hairy arms and chest. His khaki pleated twill pants accented his thighs and full basket as he strode toward me with confidence. My imagination ran wild with thoughts of his firm buttocks in those pants and I longed to sneak a peek when I could. It appeared obvious from the way Brad looked tonight that he wanted to impress me, and he had done so without a doubt.

As we met, and embraced, I was careful not to spill my red wine on him. My senses detected his cologne ... he was wearing my favorite, Este Lauder's "Pleasures." I wondered if I should take all this to be an omen of what the night might hold in store for the two of us.

"Come in, Brad ... how was the drive over? ... Would you like some wine ... red or white?" I was nervous and talking way too much and too fast.

"I'll have what you're having, Tony ... thanks."

"Oh, and in case it wasn't obvious from the expression on my face, you look very nice tonight, Brad. You always did have a very classy way of wearing your clothes ... of course the chiseled body helps a lot with that too."

Oh my gawd, was I being too forward flirting with him? I didn't want to scare him off before we even left the house.

"Thanks, Tony. You look very nice tonight as well. I've been so looking forward to this evening but to be honest, I still want to spend some time with you alone without the other guys around. I think we have a lot of catching up to do and there are some things I want to share with you."

"Yeah, I know what you mean, but I felt since this dinner with Patrick and Frank was already planned, it was a good opportunity to get together. I just hope you can put up with Patrick and I hope he's not too rude to you."

"I'm sure it will be fine, Tony. Don't worry."

"When you get back from Phoenix, Brad, we can plan another date, just the two of us, and have some time to talk."

We visited a while and the time got away from us. Our reservation was for 7:30 and it was already 7:25 when I suggested we'd better get going as I was sure Patrick and Frank would be at the restaurant early. The cool, clear night air felt good as we walked the five blocks from my condo to Martini Above Fourth. Ordinarily I would enjoy a relaxing stroll along the avenue of storefronts in route to the Hillcrest dining and nightlife. But we were running late and walked briskly to the restaurant.

We headed up the stairs to the second floor dining room that was filled with patrons and jovial conversation in the air. The large open space dining room, with soft lighting and tables shrouded with starched white tablecloths, was filled with well-dressed men. Scanning the dining room, I searched for Patrick and Frank.

We were approached by the maitre d' offering his assistance about the same time I spotted Patrick. Patrick waved to get my attention. Knowing him as I do, I could just imagine what was being said about me as I saw the expression on his face start to change.

"Frank . . . there's Tony at the reservations desk."

"Yeah, I see him; Patrick . . . is someone else with him?"

"Oh shit, is that ... is that Brad? What the hell?"

"Who? Brad?"

"It's a long story, Frank, and not one with a happy ending. ... Shit!"

We made our way through the crowd and across the dining room. As we approached Patrick, he shot me a look that could kill, but I tried to ignore it.

"Hi, guys!"

"Hey, Tony." Patrick leaned over to hug me and whispered in my ear, "What the hell are you ... ?"

"Sorry we're a bit late, guys ... the time just got away from us and we didn't allow enough time for the walk here." I realized that Frank had never met Brad and I knew I'd better take the initiative to introduce them since I felt sure Patrick wouldn't.

"Brad, you remember Patrick?"

"Yes, I do. Good to see you, Patrick."

There was only silence so I spoke up. "And this is Frank, his other half that you haven't met. ... Frank, this is Brad."

"Nice to meet you, Brad." Frank extended his hand to shake.

The four of us sat down, pulling our chairs up to the table. Patrick shot me another piercing look before he exclaimed, "Guys, if you'll excuse me, I need to use the little boy's room and I hate to pee alone, so ... Tony, would you care to join me?"

I felt like we were two grade school girls about to go hand-in-hand-by-two's to the bathroom. I knew Patrick was anxious to ream me about showing up with Brad and not saying anything to him beforehand. Patrick had never forgiven Brad for hurting me after we dated and broke up.

"Sure, Patrick!"

"Frank, would you order me another Rose Kennedy ... hold the twist?"

"Oh, and Brad," I said, "I'll have a Grey Goose 'tini, up, very dry and slightly dirty ... and three olives! Thanks."

Brad acknowledged, "That sounds good, think I'll make it two."

"We'll be right back. .... Let's go, Tony."

Before we got to the men's room I spoke up in order to get the jump on Patrick. "I know what you're thinking, Patrick, but you need to just chill out and let me handle this."

"I haven't said a word."

"You don't need to. I know you well enough to read that look on your face."

"What the hell are you doing, Tony? After the way that Brad dumped you and hurt you last time. Why would you want to put yourself through that again?"

"I'm a big boy and can take care of myself—and besides ... I think Brad has changed. He seems to have grown up since then. I plan to take things much slower this time around."

"Well, Tony, you know I'm only telling you this because I love you and don't want to see you get hurt ... again. You be careful!"

"Thanks. I will be and I appreciate your concerns, but try to understand my point of view."

"It's not going to be easy, but I'll try. *<grin>* I'll be on my best behavior tonight, I promise."

"Good. Now shall we rejoin our men at the table and enjoy the evening?"

"Sure thing," he said while we hugged before exiting the men's room.

As we approached our table, Brad and Frank were laughing and enjoying their visit in our absence, and our drinks were waiting for us. We had a wonderful evening of conversation and great food and drink. The White Party that I'd missed sounded like a wild party time in Palm Springs, and Patrick agreed that my undercover work as a nudist in a gay naturists resort in northern California sounded like a liberating experience. It flashed through my mind that for me it was more than just a fun experience. It was the discovery of a new lifestyle—one that I wanted to seek out and learn more about, starting with the many new friends I'd made at Rancho Sierra that week.

At the end of the evening, Brad and I walked back to my place and he said his goodbyes in the lobby of my condo complex with a tender kiss on my lips. He had plans to get up early the next day to drive to Phoenix, so spending the night with me was not an option. That was fine with me since I wanted to take things slow this time around.

However, I did lay awake imagining what the future might hold for the two of us. Could I be setting myself up for disappointment ... again? I couldn't help myself; I am so attracted to this man. My head began to fill with fond memories of the passion of our love making when we had been together.

In no time at all, I was fully erect and stimulated at the sexual images racing through my mind. I could almost feel the heat of passion that we inevitably created between us. Those hairy forearms and masculine hands that fondled and explored my aroused body, making me groan with pleasure. That smile of his expressing his mutual enjoyment, and those hazel eyes always fixed on my body and concerned with fulfilling my needs. I continued to feed that eroticism with thoughts of Brad to a point where I needed to take matters into my own hands. Stroking my hard cock with thoughts of Brad, it was not long before I reached a climax. Ah yes ... I needed that. Then ... I drifted off into a deep restful sleep with a pleasurable smile on my face.

∽

Over the weekend, I got a call from Brad while he was visiting his father. He just wanted to hear my voice, he said, and to tell me how much he'd enjoyed our dinner date. It was good to hear from him and I found myself imagining future plans for the two of us. I was looking forward to showing up together at Friday Happy Hour at the Top of the Park Manor. That was a popular gay men's meeting place after a long workweek, and so many good friends rendezvous there to relax and unwind.

I thought about taking Brad as my date to the next Gentlemen's Martini Night. The GMN is a social mixer for San Diego gay businessmen held at different restaurants and bars around town. It's an elite group of successful, attractive men, and there are always a lot of good friends and some very influential guys in attendance.

I thought about going with Brad to Gay Pride, and how special it would be to be seen together there as a couple. I thought about vacation plans, a cruise to Mexico, a week in Hawaii, a car trip north to Yosemite, spending time in San Francisco together. I could really show him the sights of SF if he was not familiar with "the city by the Bay."

The next week seemed to go by fast and, by Thursday evening, I knew Brad had been home for a few days. I was surprised I hadn't heard anything from him yet, but I decided to call him and see if he wanted to go together to Top of the Park Friday afternoon.

Ring, ring! "Hi, Tony."

"Hi, Brad, welcome back. Is this a good time for you?"

"Oh yeah ... sure. I've been meaning to call you, but I've been a little bummed out since I got back from my Dad's and didn't want to bring you down too."

"Why, what's wrong Brad? Is your Dad all right?"

"Well, not really. I mean he's ok, just ... ah ..."

"What is it, Brad?"

"Well, lately on the phone talking with Dad, he seemed to be a little disoriented at times but I figured I had awakened him from a nap or something else was on his mind."

"Yeah ... so?"

"Well, over the weekend being around him, I think he's started to show signs of Alzheimer's."

"Oh, gosh, I'm so sorry to hear that."

"Yeah, it can happen pretty fast and many times comes on after a traumatic experience, like my Mom's death. I think that took a lot out of him and I think we are starting to see the effects now."

"Wow! Have you talked to your brother and sister about it yet? Do you think they know?"

"No ... I've been taking some time to think this through a little and decide what I should do."

"Well, you know I'm here for you if I can help you in any way ... even if just to have someone to talk to."

"Thanks. Sometimes that's what it takes, just an ear,

someone to listen to me as I sort out my thoughts."

"Not a problem . . . any time, Brad."

"Thanks. I'll keep that in mind."

"Now . . . I think I have just the thing for you, Brad, to help you to forget about this for a while. How about going with me to the Top of the Park tomorrow evening for Happy Hour? It'll be good for you to be surrounded by your friends and people who care about you."

"Yeah . . . I don't know. You're probably right, but . . ."

"NO buts. Let's do it. It'll be good for you."

"Well . . . I think you're right. I need to get out. Do you want me to pick you up . . . say, about six o'clock?"

"Great, but just park in the basement and call me. I'll come down and we can take my car to the Park. You shouldn't have to drive after all the driving you've just done getting back from Phoenix."

"Thanks, Tony. You're a sweetheart and too good to me."

"Don't mention it. I'll see you tomorrow evening.

Look forward to it."

~

That Friday evening at the Top of the Park, we ran into many long-time friends and some old boyfriends as well. As usual, it was a festive Friday evening crowd and a beautiful balmy evening in San Diego. The sunset on the bay was awesome and very romantic from the open air bar on the ninth floor roof top. I felt very comfortable being Brad's date for the evening and having our friends notice us together again even though many of my friends still didn't understand what had happened to us or why we split up originally.

For the most part, it was the usual crowd with some of the weekend tourists mixed in. There were some HOT men in town for the mild summer weather. About midway through the evening, while Brad and I were in the middle of a lively conversation with friends, I suddenly felt a hand on my shoulder. I figured it was just another friend arriving late for happy hour and wanting to say hello. I turned to see a vision of my past flash before me.

I gasped, "Oh my gawd! Gus . . . what a surprise."

"Hey, Tony. I thought you'd be a little surprised to see me."

"A little surprised? Yeah! . . . So what are you doing now? . . . Are you here on vacation?"

"No, Tony, I live here now, as of about a year ago. I'm surprised I haven't run into you before this."

"Well, Gus, I don't go out all that much like I used to. Not as young as you."

Gus had been a bus boy at the gay-owned restaurant I'd worked at in Marin where I grew up. He was always such a hottie then and still was. I hadn't seen Gus for over five years, I guess, and last I knew he was still living up north.

"Brad! Brad … come here a minute." I called out trying to get Brad's attention. "I want you to meet someone. Brad, this is a long-time friend of mine that I haven't seen in five years or more. This is Gustavo."

"'Gus is fine … nice to meet you, Brad."

Brad extended his hand to shake. "Nice to meet you too, Gus."

"Tony and I worked together in a restaurant in northern California, a long time ago."

"Great … so do you live here now?"

"I do live here."

I interrupted their conversation. "So what do you do here, Gus … where are you working?"

"Well, Tony, you remember I attended the Culinary Academy in San Francisco when I was working at the restaurant?"

"Yeah, I do, and I knew you had several good jobs around the Bay Area."

"Well, I was never happy working in that environment with the public, and I wanted to work as a private chef some day."

"That would be a kewl job."

"Well, a friend of mine introduced me to a gentleman here in San Diego who hired me as his private chef aboard his luxury yacht."

My mouth dropped. "Wow, Gus!"

"That sounds so nice—what a great job." Brad

was impressed.

"Yeah. I'm really fortunate. Do you know who Robehr duh Sahn Cyr is?"

"The French movie director?"

"Yeah ... retired director. Well ... that's my boss!"

"Oh my gawd, Gus. That's so kewl. I'm so happy for you."

"Thanks. I really enjoy the work if you can call it that. With all the money this man has, he hosts a lot of parties on the yacht and that's the only time I have to actually work. Many times we'll just take the ship out with a few people so I can enjoy the time as well. He's a great boss."

"I'm envious."

"I tell you what, Tony. In mid-summer Robehr throws a large party on the ship. If you're interested in getting an invitation next year, I could get you on the list of guests."

"Sure, that would be really nice ... could you?"

"No problem, I want to get your contact information anyway so we can keep in touch. I'll be sure Robehr sends you an invite ... the party is by invitation only so you and Brad can be my guests on the invitations list."

"Great. How sweet of you. Do you have an iPhone, Gus?"

"Yeah, I do and I have the Bump App. Do you want to Bump and trade contact information?"

"You read my mind."

And so, through the wonders of modern technology, we transferred our personal contact information through cyber space simply by bumping our knuckles together with our iPhones in hand. I was sure this was all just a lot of talk on the part of Gus, and I was certain I would not hear a word again from him, let alone get to meet the world-renowned Robert de Saint Cyr. It would likely be another five years before our paths would cross again, I figured. But ... I was wrong!

3

Nude Beaches

With the fond memories of my nudist experience at Rancho Sierra still fresh in my mind, I vowed to seek out venues where I could meet other nudists. I felt sure many of the new friends I'd made while I was there for that one week would remain a part of my life. I now felt so comfortable in an environment free of clothing that I decided to venture out to locate our local nude beach.

For years I'd heard locals talk about "Black's Beach" and how difficult it was to get to, but that the trek was well worth it once you were there. I'd only been to a few nude beaches in my life and the last was a place called "Bad Boys Beach" near the Golden Gate in San Francisco. It was still a new experience for me then to see so many people being so comfortable going naked in public. I of course had kept my suit on and remained lying down on the beach. It wasn't until quite late in the afternoon sun that I had felt brave enough to slither my swimsuit off while remaining in a lying position and then quickly roll back over onto my stomach to avoid getting an erection.

The thought of being naked in public, along with the slight ocean breeze caressing my genitals, would have been enough to easily get me aroused if I'd thought much about it. I tried to allow myself to drift off in slumber and keep my thoughts free of anything sexual. The nude beach experience was still very new for me and now I was seeking them out to enjoy the uninhibited feeling of being free of clothing.

It was the weekend, midsummer in San Diego, so I packed my little beach bag ... lightly, as I'd been warned of the treacherous trail leading down to Black's ... and headed out by noon. Locating the wide spot in the road to park was not difficult, but the trail down to the beach did appear to be rather ominous. I was determined, however, and from the number of people I could see down below, many others had managed to climb down, so it probably looked worse than it actually was.

Ten minutes later I was on the beach and it had not been as bad of a decent as I thought. The temperature in the sun was perfect and quite a few guys were out enjoying the beach and struttin' their stuff naked in the sun. The sounds of the crashing surf, the ocean scent in the sea breeze, and the gulls screeching as they hovered above the shore line in search of food—it was all so surreal. It was like being on another planet ... a planet of nude inhabitants.

As I walked the beach in search of the perfect spot to settle, I noticed many crude man-made "beach condos" constructed of driftwood and rock that provided a wind break and a minimal amount of privacy from those beachgoers jogging or walking along the water's edge. I found a perfect spot to spread my towel and shed my clothes. I felt conspicuous applying sun protection and began to get a woodie, feeling as though I was on display and putting on a show. I stretched out on my stomach to allow my semi-erect penis to once again go flaccid and to soak up the rays of the sun. My hope was to fall asleep to the crashing sound of the waves, with the gentle ocean breeze caressing my naked body, and I began to drift off to the subtle scent of the sea life in the air.

After about an hour of slumber, I woke up with a near fully erect penis. The sun always seems to do that to me. Within minutes, it had passed. I decided to take a stroll and check out the men and to see if I knew anyone. That was certainly not likely, as I didn't really have any nudist friends other than those I had made at Rancho Sierra.

Walking along the beach stark bare-ass naked felt so free, but I could feel eyes watching me. I think likely because I was not a recognized face ... or should I say body. Sort of like fresh meat when you go to a local bar when you're new in town. At any rate, I was enjoying the attention.

The waves played tag with my feet as I walked along

the water's edge, and the feeling of the cool sand between my toes was exhilarating. There were several joggers on the beach, some of whom—although I enjoyed the sight of their large schlongs swinging side to side—made me wonder if that was painful after a while, much like a woman with large breasts jogging without a sports bra.

I found my interest captivated by the many crudely constructed beach condos, all of which appeared to be occupied. Ahead, I noticed a man standing behind the wall of his driftwood domain, watching the guys passing by. As I got closer to him, he smiled and kept his gaze on me as I walked passed. I tried to "not notice" that he had noticed. He appeared to have a toned body with an all-over tan, blond surfer cut hair. He was quite well hung and sporting a semi hard-on. The sight of him made me uncomfortably nervous. I didn't want to stare but it was hard to take my eyes off of him.

I walked on, continuing down the beach for another few hundred feet or so and had put the vision of him out of my head. There were certainly plenty of other sights to enjoy. Just the freedom of being out in the wilderness free of clothing was a liberating feeling for me that I was really enjoying.

I turned around to head back to my beach towel and once again, from a distance, I could see this same man still standing behind the walls of his domain and looking my way. Just out of curiosity, I decided to walk up from the water's edge, closer to the beach dwellers, to get a better look at this seemingly HOT man.

To my delight, his muscular body appeared even sexier the closer I got. Besides his golden all-over tan, his hair was sun streaked, and a rippled stomach with firm pecs covered by a slight bit of short blond hair glistened in the sun. His full un-cut cock was seemingly growing even more erect with each step I took.

Now, only a few feet from him, he smiled at me and waved his hand clutching his sunscreen lotion, motioning me to come over toward him. I was now semi-aroused as well and walked closer, to see what it was that he wanted, although his message was becoming poignantly clear to me.

"Hey . . . could you rub some sun block on my back for me?"

His request seemed relatively harmless and innocent. "Sure!" I responded.

I stepped into his condo and he laid face down on his towel in front of me. We were now hidden from the view of those walking along the beach. With his legs spread apart, his semi-firm cock was now visible between his thighs. I knelt down between his legs and with a handful of lotion, began to rub his muscular, broad shoulders and back. I was now fully erect and enjoying the body contact. My penis rubbed against his buttocks as I reached to massage his back and shoulders, and I could feel the lubrication from my own pre cum. It felt good, and from the low moaning sounds he was making he was enjoying the feeling as well.

His buttocks muscles began to flex and he squirmed, letting me know he was enjoying the feeling of my touch on his well lubricated body. I slid my hands down between his legs with the vision of his hard cock before me. With another handful of lotion, I began to rub his muscular buttocks and thighs. My hands spread his cheeks and fingered his anus, and he responded almost instantly. My index finger was consumed by his hungry hole. The manipulation of his prostrate now seemed to take him almost to orgasm. His ass was pulsating with euphoria with my finger still inside him.

I reached down with my other hand and began to stroke his penis. He was highly aroused and appeared to be close to climax. I too was very close even without ever having touched myself. Suddenly he rolled over to expose his engorged, erect cock.

His body now tense from near ejaculation, I should have known better than to do what I did next. My mouth consumed his hard cock and I began to deep throat him. It was just so natural to do at that moment that I didn't hesitate. I intended to tease him a bit with my mouth and finish him off with a hand job to ejaculation. I wanted to see his white cum shoot all over his tanned hairy chest and rub it in like I'd done with the lotion.

What I didn't realize was that he was so close to

climax, it only took a couple of swallows of his cock and he shot his full load in my mouth. This was something I was not used to and never enjoyed, so I immediately spat out his load into the sand. He lay there in ecstasy and my erection quickly went south. After a brief moment, he jumped to his feet, taking the sun block lotion from me.

"Hey ... thanks, man. It's so hard to put lotion on your back when you're here at the beach by yourself."

Talk about your wham bam. Not even an exchange of first names or an alias. It was strictly sex ... and one-sided at that. I do still have the memory of that erotic encounter and his hot body, and often recall that vision to this day when masturbating. Better than watching a porn movie, but not by much.

I walked back to my beach towel and lay down, quickly falling in and out of sleep. I kept thinking of this sexual interlude and how erotic it was but how sleazy I felt at the same time. I thought about Brad, and since we were not in a committed relationship, I didn't feel guilty about what I had just done. It did, however, make me want a commitment from him even that much more. I wanted to be able to say, to myself and the world, that I am in a committed relationship and we are monogamous. It was certainly much too early to approach Brad with such a proposal since we had just started dating again. But Brad appears to have matured from the first time that we dated and I feel sure I've changed as well. I hoped that this time we would find that we were compatible. There was certainly no loss of the sexual chemistry between us.

❧

I enjoyed every weekend all summer at Black's Beach because Brad was teaching summer school at the University and was attending class himself on Saturdays. Brad is a Philosophy Professor at UCSD and was taking classes to earn his Doctorate Degree in Philosophy. I have to chuckle at the thought of calling him Doctor Brad Fisher. The degree would be beneficial to his career, bringing him a much larger paycheck every month in addition to the doctoral designation added to his name.

For a long time I couldn't understand why Brad continued to rent a small apartment and had never bought a place to call home. The only benefit I could see was that his apartment was only a few blocks from campus within easy walking distance. I learned why quite by accident one evening over dinner with friends.

It was at the end of the summer. I had planned to leave the beach early this particular Saturday and while heading out, I happened to run into Cris and Michael, my nudist friends whom I had met at Rancho Sierra.

"Hey, guys. What a surprise to see you."

We embraced on the beach. Michael said, "I told Cris from way down the beach that I recognized your hot

Italian tanned bod ... but he didn't believe me."

"Oh, Michael, you're too kind. ... So what are you guys doing in town? ... A little vacation?"

"Well ... Michael and I spent a few days in Palm Springs at Triangle Inn and we just thought we'd take a couple more days in San Diego before we head back to Sacramento."

"We just got here today and we did plan to call you, Tony. Cris kept reminding me, 'Let's call Tony.'"

"Well, I'll let you guys off easy, as I was about to chew your ass for not letting me know you're in town. ... We should get together for dinner while you're here. What are you doing tomorrow night?"

"No plans ... right, Michael?"

"Well, let's get together and you can meet Brad. He and I have been dating for about three months now and he's such a sweetheart ... love to have you meet him."

"Great!"

"We'll take you to Baja Betty's. On Sunday nights it isn't usually too crowded and it's a festive place with a lot of energy ... and a lot of 'eye candy' with all the college boys that hang out there. Have you guys been?"

"Never been there but it sounds like fun. ... What time should we meet you there?"

"Let's meet in the bar at seven o'clock. You know where the restaurant is located?"

"I do," Cris spoke up. "We walked by it last time we were in town. There was a large crowd of people waiting on the street for a table and inside it was crazy. Looks like a popular place—and great food, I hear."

"Ok, we'll see you there tomorrow evening. Looking forward to it and visiting with you guys."

"And we look forward to meeting Brad too. Take care, Tony."

"Bye, guys . . . see you tomorrow."

The next evening we met up with Cris and Michael at the bar at Baja Betty's, and within a half hour, our name was called for a table. It was busier than I expected for a Sunday.

Brad seemed to enjoy our conversation with Cris and Michael and the feeling appeared to be mutual. The evening was going along very well and, at one point, Michael made a comment about how much he enjoys Mexican food. "I love good Mexican food . . . but I especially enjoy authentic Mexican food more so than the 'Americanized' version."

"Well, if you enjoy good authentic Mexican food, I can take you to some great places in Puerto Vallarta," Brad offered.

"In fact," he continued, "you know what would be an enjoyable time is if the four of us could go to PV some time on vacation. We could stay at one of my condos so the accommodations wouldn't cost us anything."

My mouth dropped open and I just looked at Brad with a blank stare. I had no idea. So this is how he was investing his money!

Michael was impressed. "Wow, Brad. That would be kewl. So you own a condo in PV?"

"Actually, Michael, I own two condos ... located in the hills above Old Town PV. One is two-bedroom and the other three, but they are vacation rentals and are rented out most of the time."

"That's great, Brad!"

I was still speechless and just listened to the details unfolding.

"If I ever want to use either of the places, I just need to block out my vacation time to be sure it's available to us. We should do that."

"Michael," said Cris, "wouldn't that be nice? We could spend the days on Blue Chairs Beach and at night we could check out the gay bars."

"That won't take long, Cris, as there aren't that many gay bars in PV and they seem to come and go pretty quickly there," Brad said. "What do you think, Tony? Wouldn't that be a fun vacation?"

Our conversation was sounding a lot like two couples making vacation plans for the future. Did I dare to allow myself to think Brad was starting to think of us in terms of a long-running relationship?

I gained control of my emotions and tried to get the shocked look off my face, and said, "Sounds like a great vacation and it would be special to do that with you and

Michael, just the four of us."

We had an enjoyable evening over dinner. Probably the best part for me was that I learned something more about Brad that night. I was surprised and a bit disconcerted that he'd never brought this up to me before, but at least now I knew why he had never invested in real estate in San Diego. Or ... had he? Since this was a new revelation to me, I wondered if there was more to discover about this mystery man that I thought I knew. He actually may own property in San Diego and I just didn't know it. Hell ... for all I know, he could own the elite Balboa Towers across from the park. You never know ... a regular Donald Trump.

4

Out of the Closet

By the end of summer, Brad and I had been dating exclusively for more than four months. The relationship was growing ever stronger the more time we spent with each other. The thought of asking Brad to move in with me had crossed my mind several times, but I wondered if he might feel it was too soon for us or if maybe he enjoyed having his own space. As it was, he rarely stayed the night at my place, usually giving the explanation of having to get to his office early in the morning and not wanting to fight the commute traffic.

It was a crisp early-November morning, and I was daydreaming at my desk. "Tony? ... Tony? Sorry to bother you, but you have a call from Brad. ... Shall I put him through?"

"Oh ... thanks, Jenn, sorry! Yes, yes, please do. Thanks."

"Hey, Brad."

"Hey, Tony. Is everything all right?"

"Yeah ... sure. Why?

"Well ... you sound a little distant. And I tried calling your cell phone but the voice mail never picked up."

"Oh, I'm fine. I was just drifting off daydreaming, and my phone battery died so I left it home charging today."

"Okay ... just checking on my Hon to make sure you're all right."

"Thanks, Babe. I'm fine ... just trying to get motivated here and get into some of the work on my desk."

"So, Tony ... you still interested in going to the Holiday Gentlemen's Martini Night this Friday?"

"That's right! This is the Osetra evening for GMN. I don't want to miss that."

"That's what I thought. It should be a festive evening. And ... if you let me spend the night, I'll take you to brunch Saturday at Moe's in the Hillcrest."

"Brad, you hardly have to bribe me to spend the night, but I'll take you up on that. Sounds like a plan."

"Great, Tony. Then I'll come by Friday about six o'clock with my overnight bag ... look forward to the evening with you."

"Thanks, Babe. I look forward to seeing you too. Thanks for calling. Hope your day goes well."

"Thanks, Hon ... you have a good day too."

Brad and I were out four and five times a week for some party or social function, or just for dinner. It was becoming a very comfortable arrangement but I wanted more. Maybe this weekend would be a good time to talk to Brad about moving in and see what his thoughts were.

Buzz, buzz! My phone signaled a call from Vinnie. This was usually not a good sign.

"Yes, Vinnie?"

"Yeah, Tony, can you step into my office? I want to go over something with you."

His request was out of the ordinary, and I wondered if it might be another challenging undercover assignment like my nudist adventure in northern California.

"Come in, Tony . . . sit down."

"You have me worried, Vinnie."

"Oh, this is not a big deal. It's just something I wanted to run by you because I think you could appreciate the position I was put in and my ultimate decision."

"Okay."

"I had a call from a prospective client. This guy was calling me from Missouri. He offered the agency a lot of money to investigate his son, but I refused to take his case."

"Really?"

"This guy is a retired military man, some high-ranking jarhead, and his son is stationed here in San Diego in the Navy. He wanted me to have one of you guys tail his son to see who he sleeps with."

"What? . . . Are you kidding me?"

"No. This guy suspects his son is gay and he wanted us to find out for sure. He wanted us to watch his son's every move when he's in the social realm and report back to him what we observed, to see if his son was ... as he put it, a 'faggot.'"

"That is sick."

"Yeah, I thought so ... and I let this guy know that when I refused to take the case. I told him 'thanks, but NO thanks' and that he might try just loving his son, unconditionally. I don't think he was too happy with me."

"Damn, what can I say? It's just sick that some people still have that mentality. I appreciate you standing up for what is right and turning this guy down."

"Well, there is no way that I could support that and I just wanted you to know."

"Thanks, Vinnie."

Vinnie is a good boss and very fair. I appreciated his defense of gay issues and I admire him for taking a stance with this bozo in Missouri.

"So, Tony, how are you coming with that stake-out on the Mrs. Robinson case?"

"Well, Vinnie, I've been tailing her for three weeks now. Seems that Jack Robinson's suspicions of his wife are correct."

"Really?"

"Yeah, every Wednesday, Mrs. Robinson makes a trip to 'Cougar Town' for a little tryst with her 'Boy Toy.' Her husband is supposed to believe she is having lunch with the ladies from the racquet club, but she is actually meeting some young stud in La Jolla for lunch and then an afternoon delight at some highway dive motel."

"Busted!"

"I've got lots of pictures and I'm just wrapping up the write-up of my findings for Jack and should have this case closed in the next day or so."

"Great. Thanks, Tony. Good work."

"Sure thing, Vinnie. If that's all, I'd better get back at it and see if I can get that finished up."

The rest of the week went by fast and it was Friday already. I was looking forward to the night at Osetra. This elegant bar and restaurant always attracts some very prominent patrons and, as far as I knew, Brad had never been there.

The bar area at Osetra is awesome, but our group usually assembles on the upper mezzanine overlooking the main bar. The focal point of the crescent shaped bar is the huge, towering, three story wine sphere rack housing the restaurant's extensive wine collection. Whenever a bottle of wine is ordered by the restaurant patrons, a "wine angel" floats up on ribbons to fetch the desired wine—sometimes thirty feet in the air, much like a Cirque du Soleil act. It's totally amazing and everyone in the bar stops to enjoy the performance. I was anxious for Brad to experience this show.

We were a little late arriving for GMN as the traffic on a Friday evening during the holidays is exceptionally heavy. This holiday venue has always been very popular with the guys and I was excited to be introducing Brad to so many of my friends.

The first couple of friends I spotted were across the room, standing by a large Lalique dolphin. Brad and I made our way through the crowd to say hello.

"Hey, guys, good to see you," I said, hugging both of them.

"Hi, Tony, where have you been? We've missed you."

"Just been a little pre-occupied these days," I said, as I rolled my eyes in Brad's direction and smiled.

"Oh, we get it." <wink, wink>

"Brad, I want you to meet a couple of friends of mine, the two that I told you about earlier. This is Sam and this is Carlo. Carlo is the artist. ... This is my ... boyfriend, Brad." It felt good to introduce Brad as my boyfriend.

Brad extended his hand. "Nice to meet you guys. Tony has talked a lot about you."

"All good, I hope?"

"Of course, Carlo. You know me."

"That's what I'm afraid of, Tony."

"So, Carlo, Tony said you are an accomplished artist. ... What sort of media are you into?"

"Over the years, I've done a variety of things, but my paintings now are a layering of acrylic paint that gives a three-dimensional effect."

"Kewl, sounds interesting."

"Some people have accused me of some sort of photographic processing of my work, but it's all done by me. It does almost appear to be hyper-realistic."

"Do you paint mostly still-life, landscapes, or what?" Brad asked.

"My works vary. Some of my earlier stuff is more abstract, while some of my more recent can be called still-life, I guess. What's unique about my work is that it gives the feeling of depth or juxtaposition. You almost feel the movement of the painting, and when combined with the right lighting, it can be surrealistic.

"Stop by the studio some time and Sam would love to give you a tour of some of my special pieces. Sam works on the marketing end of my work."

"That would be great."

"Here's my card, Brad. The studio is 'Lord's Gallery.' You and Tony come in some time. I'm not there an awful lot, but if you get onto our web site mailing, we can send you a notice when we do our next art and music mixer in the gallery."

"That sounds wonderful, Carlo . . . thanks."

"Sam and I are going to work the crowd and try to drum up some sales. You guys be good and Brad, you take care of this guy. He's a good man and don't you dare hurt him." *<Ha, ha>* They wandered off making their way through the crowd.

"They seem like really nice guys, Tony."

"Yeah, they really are, and very influential in the community."

We enjoyed the jovial atmosphere of GMN and Brad marveled at the "wine angel" show all night. After meeting many friends of mine throughout the course of the evening, we finally decided to call it a night and headed home about nine o'clock. By this time, after all the scrumptious hors d'oeuvres, neither of us was hungry for a full dinner and so we opted to just go back to my place and relax with a little more wine.

It didn't take us long to get comfortable. Lounging in boxers and a tee shirt, I put on some soft music while Brad poured a couple of glasses of wine. We stepped out onto the balcony and curled up on the wicker love seat under a blanket. I love being wrapped in Brad's arms. He makes me feel so safe. Our relationship was reaching a very comfortable and content stage and it felt good.

We were just casually chatting about some of the high points of the evening, and then ... "so, Tony, what was your first experience like ... when did you come out?"

"Wow ... where did that come from?"

"Sorry, it's just something that I'm curious about, and you already know my story ... which is not all that exciting, but still, I told you about that some time ago. I just want to know you better, Tony."

"Well, how much time do you have?" <*Ha, ha*> "It's a long story but rather interesting, I would say."

"Great, I'm all ears—let me hear it."

I moved to the opposite end of the couch and we sat facing each other with our stocking feet wrapped around each other's legs.

"Well, it was my last year in college and I was still a little confused about my sexuality, but I hardly looked at myself as gay, or queer as we talked about it back then. I was dating a really nice gal named Kayla who was like my best friend. We did everything together. Our dating relationship was strictly platonic which was her rule, and that was great by me. I still couldn't see myself being sexual with a woman. I thought I was saving myself for that special woman in my life. Little did I realize then.

"After dating Kayla for about a year, she decided to move to Honolulu to explore the world some. I was devastated, losing my buddy, my best friend. We kept in contact, of course, and she'd invited me more than once to come to Hawaii and visit her. This was a chance of a lifetime—to be able to go see the Islands and to have a free place to stay with a local, or as the Hawaiians refer to them, a haole."

"What is a haole?" Brad asked.

"The Hawaiians call a mainlander who moves to the Islands a haole. Just means they are not born in the Islands, more of a transplant to Hawaii. ... So I decided to go visit Kayla and planned to stay for three weeks since my accommodations were free. That was a decision that changed my life.

"Right away, Kayla wanted to show me the night life of Honolulu and took me the first night to her favorite dance club, which was the best place in town to drink and dance—a place called 'Hula's Bar and Lei Stand.' It's an open-air bar and dance floor located under the foliage umbrella of a huge—and I mean HUGE—Banyan tree.

"Before going in, Kayla felt she needed to warn me that this was a gay bar, but was frequented by many of the straight people since it was the best bar in town with great music to dance to. It was amazing. I was awestruck by the huge Banyan tree, alive with white twinkling lights throughout its branches, and the upbeat disco music pulsating in the air. It was truly a magical place— sort of an adult theme park.

"For me, this was the first time I'd seen two guys dance together and of course the entire bar and dance floor was predominately men—and some very attractive men, I noticed! It wasn't long before I felt very comfortable in this atmosphere of guys dancing with each other and showing public affection. I even got in on some group dancing with Kayla and some of the guys, and at one point during the evening one of her friends asked me to dance. ... What the heck, I figured, and felt safe knowing he was a friend of Kayla's and she was there to keep an eye on me. Silly, I know.

"The days went by and our routine was pretty much the same. Staying out late at night and sleeping in the next morning. Heading to the beach every day and soaking up the sun. Then heading out every evening to Hula's to socialize with Kayla and her friends. I met so many gay men being with Kayla and I loved it.

"One particular afternoon, we were shopping for clothes and, while Kayla was trying on jeans, I started up a conversation with the attractive retail clerk. His name, I learned, was Brett and I felt sure he was gay. Later that week, my suspicions were confirmed when I ran into him at Hula's with his friends. I made it a point to work my way through the crowd to say hello to him. He remembered me, and that made me feel good. I would see him out partying several other times during my extended vacation.

"The next weekend came and Kayla had made plans for one of her gay friends to join us at Hula's for a night of dancing and wanted me to meet him. His name was Kris and we hit it off right away. It was a crazy night with several other friends joining us later. We had all partied a little too much but fortunately most of us didn't have far to walk home. Kris, on the other hand, lived out near Diamond Head, and since he appeared to be a bit beyond tipsy, Kayla offered him her couch foldout bed. The only problem with that was that the couch was where I was sleeping. It looked like we would be sharing a bed!

"Having consumed so much liquor, we both went sound asleep pretty fast. I felt comfortable with Kris and we slept pretty close all night but there was no touching or playing around. Waking up a couple of times during the night to pee, I realized that I didn't find it at all awkward lying next to a man."

I paused and took a breath. "I'm sorry, Brad, do you want some more wine? I get so passionate about this experience that I almost forget to breathe. Let me grab the bottle from the kitchen."

"Thanks, Hon."

"So ... where was I? Oh yeah ... the next day, Kris decided to join a group of us at the beach in front of the 'Pink Palace.' During the course of the day, I learned that Kris was flying to the Island of Maui in the morning to spend a night there visiting a friend. He asked if I wanted to join him and I was very tempted by his offer. I wanted to see as much of the Islands as I could, and since Kayla couldn't get off work, she wouldn't be able to travel with me. I'd be on my own if I wanted to see some sights.

"Kayla's friends spent the day hanging at the beach with us and by the time we left, I'd become very comfortable with Kris. He asked me again if I wanted to fly to Maui with him in the morning—and I decided to go for it. Why not—I was on vacation and wanted some adventure in my life. I had no idea how much adventure

I was about to get into.

"Kris was pleased that I was going to join him on the overnight Maui trip. He told me that his roommate was going to drive him to the airport early in the morning and, to avoid getting off the Nimitz Highway and fighting the Waikiki traffic, it would be best if I left with him that afternoon and spent the night at Cocoa Head Stables, where he lived and worked as a stable boy."

Brad was surprised by this. "Geeze! That was a bold move on your part, considering you still thought you were straight."

"Yeah, it was, but I think a part of me was reaching out for something by this time, and Kris was so nice and gentlemanly. ... We drove to Coco Head Crater into the stables and to the carriage house, where I met his roommate, Trig. His roommate was a very handsome tall Scandinavian blond with a firm muscular body.

"Kris and Trig talked over plans for dinner that night and then both decided to get cleaned up. Kris went to use the outdoor shower and Trig stripped down in front of me showing off that gorgeous tanned body. At first I was a little uncomfortable with him walking around naked but soon realized it was natural for him, and I had to admit that I enjoyed it.

"He was quite well hung, and sported a very prominent tan line from his Speedo suit. The contrast between his fair-skinned butt cheeks and his bronze tanned body was arousing to me. He left open the bathroom door in my line of sight so that I could watch him shower. I knew he enjoyed the attention I was paying him, and why not. This was all so new to me, and I was enjoying it too. Like a kid in a candy store.

"Kris came back inside from showering, wearing just a towel wrapped around him—and before I knew it, I had two naked men around me! By this time I had a semi-woodie and was glad I was clothed and sitting down. I just continued to enjoy the scenery. Kris was extremely hung, and he too had a well toned body, with an all-over tan. He apparently enjoyed a nude beach somewhere for his sun bathing.

"While they continued to get ready to go out for dinner, Trig offered me some coke. I'm glad I turned down his offer, thinking he meant a soda, because he pulled out a mirror and, with a razor blade, laid out two neat lines of cocaine for himself and Kris. With a rolled up dollar bill, the two of them snorted their lines, rubbing the residue on their gums and then threw on some clothes and we left for dinner. I was still pretty naïve at that time.

"After dinner, we drove back to the carriage house and Trig dropped Kris and me off. He made it known that he was going to go out and party with a friend and planned to be out all night and assured us that he'd see us in the morning ... early. So it was just Kris and me, alone in the carriage house, at Cocoa Head Stables.

"Kris lit a few candles and we stripped down and crawled into bed. I knew we were not headed for sleep, but I was ready for whatever might happen. As it turned out, I made the first move, and Kris responded and tenderly showed me a night of sexual passion. I felt completely comfortable experimenting with Kris and letting him guide me up to the point of climax for the both of us."

Brad sighed. "What a romantic experience for you, Tony. That's really kewl."

"Yeah, I was pretty fortunate to have found such a compassionate yet experienced man to give my virginity to. I'd always been afraid growing up that my first time would be so traumatic for me that I would probably not sleep that entire night. However, I slept like a baby after this first experience.

"The next morning, Trig picked us up in his little Fiat with the top down and I scrunched in the luggage area behind the seats. I remember cruising down the Nimitz with the tropical winds blowing through my hair and the radio turned up, listening to Chicago singing 'If You Leave Me Now.' I was trying to sort out in my head what I had just experienced, but I was looking forward to a good time in Maui.

"In Maui, Kris and I talked and I told him I was glad we'd had our sexual rendezvous, but I needed time to sort things out in my head and didn't want it to happen again this trip. He respected my request and we had a platonic fun time together.

"Kris took me to 'Little Beach' in Maui, the gay nude beach, and we had a great day in the sun. We spent the afternoon, me in my swimsuit, and Kris, along with nearly everyone else, comfortably naked in public. We connected with Kris's friend after leaving the beach and that night we all went to dinner in Lahaina to the Old Whaler's Inn, a locals' favorite.

"I'll never forget that evening. After finishing dinner we made our way to the old wooden stairway leading down to the first floor to exit onto the beach. On the way out, Kris stopped to talk to someone seated at a table by himself and introduced me to Boz Scaggs! I was star struck!

". . . And that is pretty much it."

"Wow, what can I say, Tony? That's an amazing and romantic experience for your first time."

"Yeah, I feel pretty lucky. ... One more thing that happened to me on that trip—this happened on my last night after three weeks in Hawaii. Kayla and I went out to celebrate that night at Hula's as usual. We enjoyed the evening of partying and merriment, and when the last call for alcohol came and the last dance started to play, I found myself standing next to Kayla on my left and my store-clerk friend Brett on my right side. I knew I should ask Kayla to dance since she was supposedly my girlfriend and of course had been my gracious host for three weeks, and this was the last dance of the evening. I looked to my right at Brett, and then to my left to Kayla and then turned back to Brett and said, 'Would you like to dance the last dance with me?'

"It was at that moment that Kayla's growing suspicions about me were confirmed. She knew I was gay even before I knew it, and she was happy for me.

"Getting on the plane to come back to the mainland the next day, I cried. I didn't want to leave the experience of a lifetime, but I knew this was just the beginning for me, and that I had a lot more experiences ahead of me. I considered myself very fortunate indeed."

"Thanks, Tony," Brad said as he finished his wine and stretched with a sigh. "What do you say we get to bed and make some experiences of our own?"

"Sounds good to me!" I knew what he had in mind . . . and I sure knew what was on my mind.

5

Night of Passion

From the look in Brad's eyes, I could tell he had something more on his mind than going to sleep. When he lit the two candles in the bedroom, one by the bed and the other on the chest of drawers across the room, I couldn't help but recall the anticipation I'd felt that first night of sex that I'd had in Hawaii with Kris. Brad had me aroused as he moved slowly about the room like a cat stalking its prey. In the flickering light of the candles, this sexy man, whom I'd slept with many times in the past, made the moment feel like my very first time again. It was obvious that my sexual experience in Hawaii had sparked a flame within Brad.

"I'm yours tonight, Brad. ... You're such a sexy man, you drive me friggin crazy. You know that?"

We slipped into bed, our hot bodies between the cool, satin sheets. His hand cradled my neck and head as he kissed me tenderly, mouth exploring mouth. His tongue began thrusting deep, and I could feel the heat of passion that was so familiar to me with him. Grasping hold of his hairy forearms sent me into a full erection. With my boxer shorts now being too confining, I managed to squirm out of them. Lying naked next to him, my firm cock waiting, longing for his touch, my heart began beating faster.

I pulled his body close to mine, and ran my hands thru his chest hair, massaging his firm pecs. Sliding my hand down his fuzzy pathway to paradise and into his shorts, I grasped his hard cock with a firm squeeze and felt him pulse. He rolled over on top of me. My hands slid down his back and grasped his hairy butt cheeks as I eased off his boxer shorts. Our naked bodies locked in a passionate embrace; I was ready to give myself to him.

Then suddenly he sat up, straddling my thighs and took both of our cocks together in his hand in a slow sensual stroke. The feel of the flesh of his hot cock sliding up and down with mine, lubricated with pre-cum, nearly made me shoot my load right then.

"Oh yeah, that feels so nice ... love the feeling of our two cocks rubbing together as one."

With his other hand, he began manipulating my nipples. It felt amazing and the pleasure took me nearly to ejaculation. The vision of him straddling me, rubbing against me with his sexy, hairy chest, now taut from his own testosterone rush, brought me almost to climax several times. ... I managed to hold back because I didn't want this feeling to end.

My buttocks pulsated in anticipation of his hard cock. Brad knew my body well, how I enjoyed the feel of him thrusting inside me—hot and hard, until it would scream for release. Reaching to the floor at the side of the bed, he produced a tube of KY and slowly and sensually began to lubricate his cock while I watched and waited, the act itself making me throb.

Then, with his fully lubricated and hard cock in one hand, he raised my legs and spread them wide. He began to slowly finger my hungry anal cavity, taking his time, making me moan with pleasure. I thrust my hips forward and clinched my butt cheeks. Brad could tell I was ready and wanted him. Moving his torso into position, I could feel the head of his cock pushing, probing to penetrate me. With both my hands grabbing his butt cheeks, I pulled him in and felt his cock being swallowed up ... it felt so good.

Brad began to thrust his pelvis, slowly at first, then harder, faster, recklessly pounding my ass. I could feel him deep and thick inside me. I was stroking my cock, trying not to climax too soon. The euphoric feeling of him inside me made it nearly impossible to hold back the pressure that was building up. ... I could see Brad's muscles becoming tense, his veins prominent on his chest and neck the more he pounded. His face was flushed, perspiration forming on his forehead. He was close to cumming, his pounding and thrusting was becoming more forceful and intense, and I was losing control.

"Oh, fuck … I'm gonna cum!"

Suddenly, he pulled out and began to stroke himself to climax as I did the same. His powerful strong legs now firm with the testosterone rush clinched my body much like a boa constrictor with its prey. I heard the groan coming from deep inside him, and the intensity of his ejaculation put me over the edge almost simultaneously, shuddering as the pleasure shot through me. I felt the warm drops of white cum dapple my chest as we both shot our load.

"Ah … damn that was so hot. Mmmmmmm. You have such a sexy tight ass, Tony."

"That felt soooo good, Brad."

Our two hot loads became one pool on my chest as the two of us exhaled, both of us sweaty, glowing from torrid sex. No matter how many times we made love to each other, no matter how many ways, it always seemed exciting and new. It was like making new experiences of our own. No one else had ever brought me to where Brad could, or leave me feeling so fulfilled. Lying side by side, me on my back, he on his stomach with his arm slung over my chest, we drifted off to sleep.

❧

The morning sun had filled my bedroom when I finally woke up and looked at the clock and realized it was already after ten. Brad had gotten up some time much earlier, as usual, and I could smell the aroma of a fresh brewed pot of coffee. I just lay there for a while thinking how wonderful it would be to wake up to this every morning for the rest of my life.

Pulling on my boxer shorts, I stumbled sleepy-eyed into the kitchen. "Well … good morning 'Sister Mary Sunshine.' How did you sleep?"

Wiping the sleep from my eyes, "I slept like a baby … how about you?"

"Great. It's amazing what good sex will do for you, right?"

"You got that right. That was amazing last night. … Oh, and Babe, thanks for pulling out before you shot your load inside me since you didn't have a … 'raincoat' on."

"Of course, Tony … I'd never do that until we've had a chance to discuss it."

"You're a sweetheart."

"So, are you ready for a cup of coffee, Hon?"

"That sounds good. Thanks."

We stepped out onto the balcony into the crisp morning air and curled up on the love seat with our warm coffee. It was going to be another beautiful day. The sky was clear and blue, and in the distance we could see the ocean.

"So what time do you want to walk down to Moe's for brunch, Babe?" I had made up my mind to bring up to Brad the idea of him moving in with me.

"Should we plan on noon? ... It'll be close to that by the time we get cleaned up and get our act together."

With a yawn and stretch I responded, "Sounds good to me. That way I can have a little more time to wake up after my second cup of coffee."

"Sleepy head! I don't know if you felt my eyes on you this morning. When I woke up, I just lay there next to you, watching you sleep."

"Oh great ... probably with my mouth open and snoring. Not a pretty picture, I'm sure."

"Not at all. You were like a sleeping Adonis next to me. I had to pinch myself to believe this was all really happening to me."

"Aw ... you are too sweet."

We showered together and nearly got too sidetracked to make our brunch plans. We did manage to cool it down and after getting ready, headed off to Moe's. I love living in this little enclave in the Hillcrest, being able to walk to most everywhere. We got seated at a quiet corner table on the back patio and had our first mimosa before ordering brunch. This was a great spot for me to make my proposal to Brad. I was nervous, but the mimosa would take the edge off of those nerves.

"So, Brad, last night was awesome, starting with our

night out with GMN and ending with ... well, you know."

"Yes, it was very enjoyable and always so comfortable being with you. You make me feel good about myself the more I get to know you the stronger my affections are for you."

Okay, here I go. "So ... I was just thinking ... do you think maybe we should do this all the time?"

"You mean brunch?"

"No, silly. I mean would you consider moving in with me, living together, the two of us?"

"Wow! I have to say the thought has crossed my mind—and to be honest, especially after last night, that's exactly what I was thinking about while I was making the coffee this morning."

I responded sarcastically. "And ... have you made your decision ... thinking about it?"

"I was waiting to hear what you wanted and now that I know, I can tell you ..."

Brad reached for his champagne flute and raised it as if making a toast. "I can tell you, Tony, I could think of nothing that would give me more pleasure than to move in with you as your full-time partner in life and love."

"I love you. It makes me feel so good to hear you say that. I love being by your side and I'm so excited to be committing to a relationship with you, Brad. You inspire me and make me look forward to waking up each morning and spending a new day with you. You make me feel so special." We raised our glasses and took a sip before leaning across the table to kiss, which sort of made it all official.

"So when do you want to make all of this happen?"

"Before Christmas, I hope. I want to spend this holiday season with you in my life and in my home ... in OUR home."

"One thing, Tony, if you're all right with this, I want to keep my apartment near the University since my rent is so cheap, and that way I can run over there during the day if I have time to kill between classes and get some work done ... or take a nap. Are you okay with that?"

"Sure, I guess so. That way too, if we have out of town guests, we can always let them stay in the apartment if they want more than just our guest bedroom or need a little more privacy."

"Sounds great. Then I'll get my clothes and some of my other personal belongings together this next week and plan to move next weekend."

"Kewl, I'll make space for you in the closet and some drawer space as well and, of course, help you with the move. Now let's order some brunch. I'm starved."

❧

Brad was moved in well before Christmas and we enjoyed the holiday parties as a couple. The New Year came and was off to a great start.

In March, Brad graduated from the doctorate program at UCSD and overnight he became Doctor Fisher, professor of Philosophy at UCSD. I was very proud of him that he had completed this goal and glad that we could once again do things together on weekends. Spring was coming and I looked forward to nature walks, beach trips and long bike rides through Balboa Park. I was also hoping to introduce Brad to the naturist community by getting him to join me this summer at Black's Beach.

With the spring came more health problems for Brad's Dad in Phoenix. His ALZ had escalated and then he fell and broke his hip. He was in and out of the hospital and Brad was taking a lot of trips to see him. After fighting to come back from his hip surgery, his Dad had come down with pneumonia, and four weeks later, passed away. I was glad I was there for Brad during this difficult time.

Between Brad and his siblings, an older sister married with children and younger brother, single, they managed to get the service behind them and get the assets in the family trust divided among them. I think Brad was a little shocked at how much his inheritance was and he promised to take me on a long vacation as soon as we could plan the time off together. One thing he did for himself with his windfall was to trade in his old BMW for a new 335i hardtop convertible BMW. That was something he had wanted for a long time, and he looked so sexy behind the wheel with the top down, cruising around downtown San Diego.

I felt my life was also going well. Just the fact that I had Brad in my life was fulfilling for me. But aside from that, I was quickly becoming the most senior Investigator in my office. Having been assigned some rather complicated cases recently, my boss, Vinnie, had recognized my abilities again with yet another promotion within the firm. I was still waiting for the opportunity to investigate a high profile murder case—something like the case I'd solved in northern California—but that would come in time.

Just after the first of the year, I was asked to run for the Gay Businessmen's Chamber of Commerce. There were only two open positions and three candidates, and I was elected to serve a two-year term! I was enjoying the political involvement of my community. This could actually be the start of an entire political side-career for me.

We were fast becoming a prominent couple in the city and I loved my new life with Brad.

6

A Memorable Affair

I could hear the front door close and I knew Brad was home. It was early summer and the two of us had settled into a comfortable living arrangement. Many days of the week, Brad would make it home before me, but today I'd left the office early and was sitting on the balcony when he arrived.

"Hey, Hon, how was your day?"

I was pretty much still in a daze from reading what had arrived in the mail, and could barely speak. "It was good. How about you?"

"It was a little stressful today—getting close to finals, you know. I'll be glad when this school year is over and I can look forward to a new one."

"Look at this, Brad. ... It came in the mail today. I'm still in shock from reading it." I handed Brad the linen embossed formal invitation.

Monsieur Robert de Saint Cyr
requests the honour of your presence
aboard his luxury yacht GODY-GO
in celebration of "le 14 Juillet," Bastille Day.

The ship will leave promptly from the Large Ships pier,
slip 139-A at 8:00 p.m. on July 13.
Admittance will be by invitation only
for this black-tie affair.

Valet parking is provided and recommended.
Fireworks off the stern of the ship at midnight
and guests can expect to be returned to the pier
no later than 1:30 a.m.

RSVP Regrets only.

"This is the guy that Gus works for, right?"

"Yes! Yes, the famous Director, Robert de Saint Cyr. You know, *Still Waters Run Deep*, his last movie before his retirement . . . the one that won so many awards that year?"

"Yeah, I do remember that. Wow."

"Yeah, WOW. Can you imagine us attending one of his parties?"

"Well, I recall Gus saying he was going to put you on the guest list for the party this year."

"I know, but I never really expected he'd do it! This is so

exciting. . . . I hope I can still fit in my Calvin Kline tux."

"Looks like I might have an opportunity to use mine finally. I'd better make sure it still fits me as well and we should probably have both of them cleaned."

We were both thrilled about this once in a lifetime opportunity to "hob knob" with such special party guests. We imagined there could be a lot of film industry guests and possibly some actors in attendance as well. I was also looking forward to seeing Gus again and sampling some of his gourmet hors d'oeuvres.

The time seemed to go by fast and before we knew it, July 13 had arrived. Brad and I started early that afternoon with the primping and the usual fussing to make sure we were "dressed to the nines" for the party. We wanted to make sure we blended in with the rest of the guests. By the time we were ready to walk out the door, we both looked fabulous.

We left the house plenty early since we weren't sure where the Large Ships pier actually was, but figured it certainly couldn't be that difficult to locate. Having the valet parking would be convenient too. We decided to take Brad's new BMW since it would surely make a better impression than my Honda Civic. I would have loved to pull up with the top down, but we didn't want to get our hair blown after all the time we'd spent getting our coifs to look just perfect.

"There it is, Brad . . . see the sign, *'Large Ships'*?"

"Okay, I guess we just look for the slip number or for the valet parking."

Ahead we noticed several cars lined up, and figured that must be the valet parking drop area. When we noticed the many Bentleys, Rolls Royces and other luxury cars, we felt sure we were in the right place.

A young attractive man dressed in a pink tux shirt with a black vest and black pants approached the car. "Welcome, guys. I assume you're here for Mr. de Saint Cyr's party?"

"Yes, thank you," Brad said as he handed his keys to the young man.

"No problem. Be sure you have your invitation with you and just follow the pier out to where you see the red and blue balloons and the crowd of people boarding his ship."

"Thanks." "Thank you." Brad and I echoed each other.

I had butterflies in my stomach. We walked a short distance on the pier before noticing the crowd queuing up to board a yacht that was absolutely amazing.

Standing in line, we made small talk with the couple directly in front of us and found out why the line had backed up. Seems there had been some sort of confrontation with a man and woman not on the guest list who'd tried to board the ship. They'd been escorted out by security, but only after a lot of resistance on the part of the gentleman, who was no match for the big bouncer-type musclemen.

As Brad and I waited in line, I happened to notice a homeless man on the pier, huddled near the compressor motor of an ice machine. I felt bad for him, seeing all the decadence of these party-goers, and here this poor man was trying to keep warm outside in the open sea air. He appeared to be comfortably snuggled up to the warmth radiating from this machine. It was as if he had done this countless times before, but perhaps never with this much fanfare around him.

We finally made it to the front of the line and boarded the ship at the bow on the upper deck. We were welcomed aboard with a brief description of the yacht and its safety features before we were turned loose to enjoy the party. The ship, according to the concierge, was a 175 foot Ferretti custom, and cost approximately seven million. With over 2,800 square feet of living area, each of the five cabins has its own bath and three of those boast a private in-room Jacuzzi. The promenade deck features a marble ballroom floor with home theater, Dolby surround sound, and of course the unique baby grand piano made especially for Mr. de Saint Cyr. The rear sun deck, he explained, made of highly polished teak wood, is perfect for nude sun bathing and outdoor entertainment with the built-in gas stainless barbeque island. The upper most deck, the observation deck, is where the twenty-four man Jacuzzi is located with a panoramic view of the sky at night.

It was totally awesome. Brad turned to me and whispered, "Must be nice to be rich."

"Someday, Babe, I'll buy you a yacht, too."

We entered the promenade deck through the double doors opposite the dock side where the party was already under way. My mouth dropped opened in awe when we walked in. We descended a large, curved stairwell down to the ballroom dance floor where guests were mingling while sipping champagne. Across the floor, an attractive black man in white tails was seated at a piano playing show tunes. This was no ordinary piano, aside from the fact that it was a baby grand. This was a flamingo pink lacquered baby grand. The concierge's reference to "unique" now made sense and was quite the understatement. I'd never seen a baby grand in anything but black or white.

"Welcome aboard, gentlemen," a waiter passing by greeted us. "Would you care for a glass of Dom Perignon or something from the bar?"

"Thank you, I'll have some champagne. Brad?"

"Sure, champagne sounds good."

I felt a little more comfortable now with a drink in my hand, and I began to scan the crowd for any familiar faces. I never expected to see anyone I knew other than

Gus, but across the room—watching our every move until our eyes met—I spotted Carlo and Sam, our friends from Gentlemen's Martini Night.

"Look, Brad. There's Carlo and Sam. Let's go say hello. What a shock to see them here."

"Hey, guys! Nice to see you both." I reached out to hug Carlo and then Sam. "You guys remember meeting Brad?"

"Yes, we do. ... Glad to see someone we know here. We've been on 'star-search' but so far no one we recognize."

"So, Carlo, how is it that you guys know Robert ... ah, Mr. de Saint Cyr?"

"Well, Robert commissioned me to do a painting for the foyer of his La Jolla home at the beach. Ever since then, we've been invited to this annual party."

"How nice."

"Yes, it is. ... And how is it that you guys know Robert?"

"Actually I don't know Robert personally, but I'm friends with his personal chef on the yacht, Gustavo. I'm so thrilled to be invited to the party this year."

We continued to check out the arriving guests, and we estimated there were about forty or so aboard the ship not counting the staff which probably numbered ten or more. We'd heard rumors of famous directors and producers aboard but no one we recognized yet.

Shortly before departure from the pier, we noticed director Quentin Tarantino making his way through the crowd. I guess the famous people arrive fashionably late.

We then spotted Ellen DeGeneres and Portia, and from Robert's last big award-winning movie, his leading man, Kiefer Sutherland. I'm sure there were other movie industry people in attendance, but these were a few of the more recognizable guests that Brad and I were able to spot in the crowd.

At five after eight we felt the ship start to pull away from the dock. The party was officially under way. We joined Carlo and Sam out on the rear deck of the yacht to watch the shoreline disappear as we headed out to sea.

The music played on and we laughed and partied as the champagne continued to flow. Gus's special hors d'oeuvre creations of bacon wrapped scallops, crab stuffed mushroom caps, canapés of smoked duck and more, were circulated by formally attired waiters and set out on an exquisite buffet table accented with a huge shimmering dolphin ice sculpture lighted from below. A large seashell filled with Beluga caviar was positioned at the center of the table flanked with triangles of Melba toast, Blinis Russian pancakes, and a variety of crackers. Large serving platters of crab cakes, asparagus wrapped in prosciutto, apricot with boursin cheese, chicken tenders in peanut sauce and Vietnamese egg roll completed the buffet table. This was the most exclusive, over-the-top party I had ever attended and it was nice to be sharing this experience with Brad. We still had not seen or met Robert, but the night was young and I figured he was waiting for the right time to make his entrance and greet his guests.

"Carlo," I said, "if you see Mr. de Saint Cyr, do you think you could introduce him to us? We've yet to meet him."

"Sure, it would be my pleasure. He's a very nice and easy-going individual. You'll like him."

"I'm sure there are a lot of big names on the guest list, but I only recognize a handful. I overheard someone say a while ago that the writers from the *Dynasty* TV series are aboard."

"Oh, yeah, I was just talking to them. Would you like to meet them, Tony?"

"Oh my gawd, I'd love to. I loved that show. ... My boyfriend at that time, Kerry, and I would make sure when *Dynasty* came on that we were in bed watching the show with a martini in our hand. We would wait for Alexis to take a drink and we would follow. It was a quirky tradition, every Thursday night."

<*Ha, ha*> "That's too funny! I'm sure the Pollocks would love to hear that story. There they are inside, seated near the piano. Let's go meet them if you're up to it. Sam, Brad, excuse us for a moment."

"Sure thing."

We walked inside and approached the elderly couple seated. He was a very dapper, distinguished gentleman, and she was a dignified, elegant woman with perfectly coiffed hair. "Excuse me," said Carlo. "I'd like to have you meet a good friend of mine. This is Tony Felice. Tony, this is Robert and Eileen Pollock."

I knelt down in front of them to position myself at eye level with the two of them much like I would if greeting royalty. "It is such a pleasure to meet you. I was such a fan of *Dynasty.*"

They loved hearing of my weekly tradition watching the show with Kerry. I felt sure they must have heard many similar stories over the years, but to me it was a special memory I wanted to share with them. We made some small talk and then I left them to enjoy their evening. Meeting the two of them was certainly a highlight of my evening.

Carlo and I joined Brad and Sam right where we had left them by the food. By this time, Robert de Saint Cyr was mingling with the guests and headed our way.

"A very good evening with you, gentlemen!" Robert greeted us with a hint of a French accent.

"Hello, Mr. de Saint Cyr."

"It is Mr. Carlo and ... Mr. Sam, no? Correct?"

"Yes, sir. Very good memory considering we only see you once a year."

"Oh ... the mind seems to go a little more with time, but *c'est la vie.*"

"I'd like to have you meet a couple of friends of ours ... this is Tony Felice and Brad Fisher."

Robert nodded his head. "It is with much pleasure,

welcome to my Bastille affair. Please enjoy."

I extended my hand. "It's such a pleasure to meet you, Mr. de Saint Cyr."

"Please, you call me Robert and I call you Tony."

"Robert ... your personal chef, Gustavo has been a close friend of mine for years."

"Ah yes, you know Mr. Gustavo? Good man he is, very much talent with the food, I enjoy him very much. I remember he speak of you and insist that I invite you to my affair ... so, welcome."

"Thank you, Robert."

"I must greet my friends now, but I want that you both enjoy this evening. We can talk more later, no?"

"Thank you."

Robert was a very tall gentleman with a full head of silver tousled hair. He seemed very jolly and friendly, with a twinkle in his eye. He seemed like the kind of guy who never met someone he didn't like. It was easy to feel very comfortable with him.

Midnight seemed to come around fast and, as promised, the GODY-GO was anchored far out at sea and the fireworks display was launched from the stern of the ship. With the ship now anchored, the four of us decided to go up to the observation deck and find a seat around the Jacuzzi to view the show. It was awesome to be snuggled next to Brad in our complimentary commemorative blanket, with our glasses of champagne, the music, and now fireworks to light the midnight sky. It was all so surreal and I felt very privileged and blessed.

Once the fireworks were over and Robert said a few words to his guests using the PA system, we began the journey back to the pier. The night was quickly coming to an end—but what a memorable evening it had been.

By 1:15 a.m. we were docked. With so many people now wanting to leave the ship and get to their vehicles, Brad and I decided to hang around with Carlo and Sam for a bit and let the crowd diminish. Besides . . . we didn't want this evening to end—it was all so fabulous.

"Hey, Brad . . . before we leave, I'm going to slip into the galley and see if Gus is still around and thank him for this evening and his wonderfully delicious creations."

"Sure, Tony. No problem, I'll be here with Carlo and Sam and maybe when you get back we can look for Robert and thank him before we head out too."

I made my way to the front of the promenade deck and the swinging galley doors. By this time, many of the guests had left and I hoped it wouldn't be a problem to pop in on Gus.

The galley kitchen was very quiet, but then I heard what appeared to be an argument taking place at the opposite side around the corner from the walk-in box. I could hear two men talking loudly and one of them appeared to be agitated. I hesitated to interrupt, but I realized the other man sounded like Gus and I wondered if he was in some sort of trouble.

"No ... leave me alone! I told you I'm not interested in getting involved with a cheating asshole."

"You bastard, you owe me this. You prick tease! This is just between us. No one else has to know."

"Let go, I told you NO. Now leave me alone. Get out!"

"Gus, are you in here?" I called out as I rounded the corner.

To my surprise, I found Gus was pinned against the wall by a tall Hispanic man wearing the now familiar valet parking uniform—pink tux shirt and black vest. Gus seemed to be distraught by his advances and the man pulled his arms back once he saw me approach—but not before I noticed a distinguishing forearm tattoo. He had his sleeves rolled up and while he had his arms extended, I noticed a yin-yang, black and white ink tattoo on his right forearm. He fled the kitchen almost immediately.

"Are you all right, Gus?"

"Yeah, I'm fine."

"What was that all about? It sounded pretty threatening."

"It's no big deal. He's just been pushing to get me to sleep with him but I won't do it. It's nothing, I'm fine. So did you guys have a good time tonight?"

"Oh gosh, did we ever! It was so nice and I owe it all to you. Thanks, Gus!"

"Good, I'm glad you enjoyed it. Robehr knows how to throw a party."

"And ... Gus, your food creations were just wonderful.

I don't know how you do it."

"It comes natural for me and I love doing it. Lots of practice and an unlimited budget helps."

I hugged Gus to say goodbye. Oddly, it seemed his embrace lasted longer than I would have expected, almost as if I were his savior and security blanket. At any rate, we said our goodbyes and I headed back to find Brad and start heading home.

We were one of the last people to leave the pier that night and on our way out, I noticed the homeless man sound asleep near the warmth of his compressor motor.

On the drive home, Brad and I reminisced about the highlights of the evening. I contemplated telling Brad of the scene that I'd witnessed in the galley with Gus and the valet parking guy, but I decided against it. Why put a damper on the fun evening.

"I'll get a really nice 'Thank You' card for Robert and send it out from the two of us, Brad."

"Thanks. That will be nice—and maybe it will keep us on the invitation list for next year!"

7

Discovery

Here it was, mid-week after such a memorable party and I still had not come back to reality . . . but reality was about to set in really fast.

Buzz, buzz! "Yes, Jenn?"

"Good morning, Tony . . . I have a call for you."

"Morning, Jenn. . . . Who's on the phone?"

"Well, Tony, I'm not sure but I think he said his name was D Sonceer? Does that sound familiar?"

"Not in the least, Jenn, but that's no problem. Put him through."

"Thanks . . . here you go."

"Good morning, this is Tony Felice. How can I help you?"

"Hallo and a good morning to you, Mr. Tony. It's good that I am able to find you."

I recognized that accent immediately. "Good morning, Mr. de Saint Cyr. How are you? What a pleasant surprise."

"Please, Mr. Tony, you call me Robert. ... I am holding up under my circumstances."

"How DID you track me down anyway?"

"I recall you are friend with Carlo when I meet you at my affair. I talk to Carlo to find out where it is that you work."

"Well, that is certainly some good detective work. How can I help you?"

"Please forgive, as my English it is not very good. Gustavo, my chef, he always speak well of you and you skill as detective. I want that I should hire you ... please?"

"Well, sure. I hope it's nothing serious. ... Oh and by the way, thanks again for the wonderful party. Brad and I had a fabulous time."

"It pleasures me. Now I must come to you for help. My guests at my affair was fun time ... but seems to have ended badly."

"Really? I'm not sure I understand."

"Well, Mr. Tony ... I would like that we meet so that we could speak of this and to give you money so that you can start with invest ... investigate of the situation. I pay you well for your work. Will you join me for lunch on the veranda at my house ... today if it be possible for you?"

"Yes, sure, but please fill me in a bit. What seems to be the problem?"

"I don't want that you should be upset ... Gustavo, he was murdered on my yacht some time after my affair

Saturday night."

I could feel the blood drain from my head and I felt faint. I was sick to my stomach at the thought of sweet, innocent Gus being murdered by anyone. "Oh my gawd, I can't believe it. . . . What a horrible tragedy."

"Sorry that I must be the one to break you to this unfortunate situation, but it is better that you should hear it from me and no to read it in the news. He was good man, Gus, and it is unfortunate to be without him."

I managed to hold back the emotion welling up inside me. "Yes, we all will miss him."

"It is for this reason that I want that you should work for me and my hope that I find his killer. I fear the police may be too involved to spend much time to solve the mystery of his death. My hope that this killer is found soon. You can help . . . oui?"

"I will do what I can . . . whatever it takes, Robert."

"Thanks to you, Mr. Tony. If you will come to my house at noon today, I can speak to you with more detail. You need to contact with the police for my full crime statements."

"Sounds good. I will be there."

"You are able to find me, Mr. Tony?"

"I do have the address from the invitation RSVP. I assume that is your home address?"

"Oui, it is my pleasure to host you for lunch and to begin to investigate. I want that we can catch the bastard who did this to our Gustavo."

"Fine, I will see you at your home at noon today. Thanks. And . . . my condolences to you, Robert. Goodbye."

My stomach was in a knot. I could not believe what I had just heard. It seemed like a nightmare, but I knew I was awake and this was really happening.

I called Brad on his cell phone just to talk to someone else. Apparently he was in class, and his voicemail picked up. Since we had tentative plans to meet for lunch, I needed to at least let him know that I wouldn't be able to make lunch with him.

"Hey, Babe. I want to let you know that something came up today and I've got plans for lunch after all. I'm taking on a special case and I'll tell you all about it later. It's not good, however—that much I can tell you. I'll see you at home tonight. Love you, Babe!"

I showed up at the de Saint Cyr mansion in La Jolla a bit early and was buzzed in through the security gate. I was anxious to hear more about the murder and to start formulating an investigation methodology.

I was greeted at the front door by a butler who invited me in and showed me to a wicker settee on the veranda.

"Mr. de Saint Cyr will be with you shortly. Can I get you a cocktail before lunch or possibly an ice tea or fresh lemonade?"

As much as a cocktail would calm my nerves, I settled on a glass of lemonade. It was only a few minutes later that Robert showed up and joined me for a drink before we sat down for lunch.

"So good that you should come, Mr. Tony ... and investigate Gustavo's untimely demise."

"Well, I could say it's my pleasure, but I'd much prefer that this had not even happened. Let's just say I am glad to help out in any way I can. Gus was a very special friend of mine for a long time."

"Oui, Gus was a good man, very special to many people and much talent with the food."

"So tell me what happened—at least what you know, anyway." I took out a small note pad and my gold Cross pen to make some notes.

"Surely, Tony. ... I go to the pier Monday morning so that I check on the GODY-GO. When I get there, I find she is no in her slip. I call Gustavo on his cell phone but no able to reach him."

"Did you report the yacht as missing at that point?"

"Yes, oui, even though at times Gustavo take her out, but no without letting me know or near his cell phone. It is usual after these affairs on my yacht Gustavo would sleep on board the night of the affair and clean up the next day. Gus then lock her up and be sure the ship secure."

"And did Gus remain on the yacht that Saturday night after your party?"

"My thinking that he did. I never ask ... I give my faith to him completely. When I leave the ship that night, Gustavo was still there but the guests they had left already. ... I think security men was gone and my skipper was gone not long after we dock."

"So you reported this to the police as a missing person and possibly stolen yacht on Monday afternoon? About what time was that?"

"I think once I try to locate Gustavo and had no more contacts, it was ... maybe, one o'clock or more. I feel bad that I allow so much time to go by before I contact the police. You will find all this with the interview I talk with the police."

"Yes, of course, I understand, and I'll be getting a copy of that report later."

It appeared that lunch was ready and so we moved to a shady spot in the back yard, seated at a glass top table with white wrought iron chairs. The Star Jasmine was in full bloom and smelled so sweet. Lunch was very gourmet but light and healthy—a Caesar salad with hearts of romaine, followed by crab cakes with a light aioli sauce. I thought how wonderful it would be to have servants to cook and serve you like this every day. What a life.

"So it was Tuesday when you were notified that Gus had been murdered?"

"Oui, that is correct. The police call me yesterday late morning, say the Coast Guard spotted my yacht say forty miles out, adrift at sea. They go aboard to see if there was anyone in danger, and they find Gustavo . . . dead."

Those words were still too fresh for me to hear and I nearly lost my lunch. I managed to take a drink of my lemonade and keep it down.

"When the Coast Guard find Gustavo was dead, they secured my ship to protect evidence. GODY-GO she was towed back to the pier for that the police could investigate."

"I would assume this is under the jurisdiction of San Diego Police Chief BV Tallerico?"

"That is what I know. I am still wanting for a report from police on more of the details myself."

We made some more small talk while we finished lunch and it was obvious that I needed to meet with Chief Tallerico as soon as possible to find out more details of how Gus was murdered, and any other evidence they might have that could help me with my investigation.

Robert reached into his sport coat inside pocket and pulled out a wallet. He handed me a check saying, "This should start with you on the investigate and you keep a record of you services, please. I pay you well, I do what it take to solve this and to catch the bastards."

Without looking at the check, I thanked Robert and told him I would be talking to him soon. "Thanks for lunch too. Oh, and one more thing . . . can you get me a list of all the guests who were in attendance at the party Saturday? Right now, everyone is a suspect."

"Sure, that is no problem for me, but I know my guests

could not be responsible to do something this horrible."

"I would tend to agree with you, but I still need to review the guest list as part of my investigation. Thanks."

Robert walked me out to the front of the house and I headed home to start making some notes and call Police Chief Tallerico to arrange a meeting with him.

∾

"Mr. Felice, if you hold on, I'll transfer you to Chief Tallerico now."

"Thanks."

"Yeah, this is Tallerico."

"Good afternoon, Chief. This is Tony Felice, PI with Balboa Private Investigators. I've been hired by Robert de Saint Cyr to investigate the murder of Gustavo Cabrera."

"Ah yes. Your name is familiar. What can I do for you, Mr. Felice?"

"Please call me Tony."

"Okay . . . so what is it that you want from me?"

"As part of my investigation, I'd like to come in and talk with you regarding the murder scene and also get a copy of the police report."

"Well, you know I'm awfully busy here and not sure when I can find some time for you."

"I won't take much of your time, Chief, and I'd like to come in later this afternoon, say about four o'clock, if that works for you? The sooner I get started with this investigation, the sooner we can solve the murder."

I could hear the Chief sigh at the other end. "I don't think we need your help to solve this, Mr. Felice, but if you'd like to come in this afternoon, and try to earn your money, I could find a few minutes to talk to you—and I'll have a copy of the police report ready for you."

"Thanks, Chief. I'll see you at four this afternoon."

I was not looking forward to working with Chief Tallerico as he was known to be rather homophobic, but there was no getting around it.

When I walked into the precinct, a receptionist greeted me and announced my arrival to Chief Tallerico. She then pointed me in the direction of his office where he met me at the door.

"Good afternoon, Mr. Felice. I'm not sure we've met before but as I said, I recognize the name."

"We've never actually met but I recognize you from the media."

As we sat down, he said, "Felice ... if I'm correct, you're the investigator who solved that case up north in that nudie resort last year?"

"Yes ... that was me."

"I thought so. The guys here at the precinct refer to you as the Naked Dick."

"Well, I'm not sure if I should take that as a compliment or not, but I've been called worse things in my life. I was pleased to have solved that case, however."

"Well, I think you got lucky on that one, Mr. Felice."

"I beg to differ with you on that point, but you are allowed to have your opinion. That's not why I'm here, however."

"So, Mr. Felice … along with your nickname here at the precinct, there's talk that you are … *a little light on your heels?*"

I was really getting irritated with his lack of professionalism and his insinuations. "Chief, I hardly think this interrogation of me as a Private Investigator is called for. I'm sure there are a lot of skeletons in your closet that we can drag out, *Chief 'Beverly' Tallerico.* Tell me … how did it feel wearing those pretty little dresses until you started pre-school? … And having your hair done up with pretty bows and curls?"

His mouth dropped open and he glared at me with a look of horror and disdain. "So tell me *Beverly,*" I continued, "did your parents ever get that little girl they'd wanted so badly when you were born?"

His face now flushed with anger, he darted quickly from behind his desk and closed the door to his office. "Why … you son of a b … itch!" he stammered. "How in the hell do YOU know about that? Nobody knows that."

"I'm a Private Investigator, remember? It's my job to know these things." I flashed him my best innocent smile.

"Don't you EVER bring that up again! Do you understand me? You can forget you ever heard about that."

"I just wanted to make sure we understand each other

and that you treat me with the respect I deserve. You can call me Mr. Felice and I will restrict myself to calling you Chief Tallerico. Do we have an understanding here?"

"Yes, certainly." He still seemed rather upset at the thought of me knowing of this skeleton in his closet and he paced around his desk before taking a gulp of coffee from his mug and sitting back down.

"Now if you don't mind," I continued, "I don't want to take up any more of your precious time than I have to, so let's get with the details of the murder as you know them."

"The details are all in this report, and this is your copy. But let me quickly go over what we know. Apparently one or more persons came aboard the yacht sometime early in the morning of Sunday the fourteenth. Gustavo was likely asleep on the yacht and startled by the intruders. It appears there was a struggle on the stairway leading down to the promenade deck. There was a glass display case in the stairway where Mr. de Saint Cyr had some of his trophy awards displayed. In the course of the struggle, someone fell against the case and broke the glass. The perp then grabbed one of the trophies and struck Gustavo with it.

He fell down the stairs to the marble floor below, striking his head hard at the landing. Presently we are awaiting the coroner's report to determine if the fall killed him or the blow to his head before the fall. It looks like the thugs then took the yacht out for a joy ride and tried to get rid of the body and the yacht."

"I don't understand. What do you mean 'tried to get rid of the yacht?' I thought it was just abandoned at sea, was it not?"

"It was probably abandoned about thirty miles out or so. The pirates used the dingy motor-boat to get back to shore. Before they left, they tried to sabotage the yacht to sink. They left a can of fuel near a lighted portable propane gas heater, apparently with hopes that it would heat up and eventually explode the fuel and sink the ship, taking any evidence—and the body—to the bottom of the ocean. What they didn't plan on, however, was that the propane tank was nearly empty and the flame extinguished before the fuel-can could ignite and explode. Their hasty departure in the dingy left the yacht intact and adrift at sea all day Sunday and Monday, until it was found on Tuesday afternoon."

"Interesting. I assume there were fingerprints on the murder weapon?"

"Assault object . . . and yes we do have prints. However, the fingerprints don't match any in our system's database so that's no help currently.

"Another interesting point," the Chief continued. "The dingy was found yesterday washed up on a sandy stretch of beach at the military base, Camp Pendleton. Apparently this is the point where the killers returned to land and we have some very poor footprints that seem to match some prints we were able to lift on the yacht from the blood that they stepped in. This seems like a very amateur invasion and possibly was a 'joy ride' that went wrong ... seriously wrong."

"I see. This is all very helpful, Chief. I don't want to take any more of your time now but if something else comes up that you think I should know about, I'd appreciate you giving me a call. Here's my card, and if I come up with any new information I think you should know of, I'll call you."

"Sounds good to me, and, Mr. Felice ... remember our agreement, I don't want to hear any rumors about me anywhere by anyone. Do we have an understanding?"

"Not a problem with me, as long as you watch your tongue and show me the respect I deserve as an accomplished investigator."

"And ... to answer your question, Mr. Felice ... I am an only child."

"I know that." I flashed him a smile and extended my hand to shake as I prepared to leave his office. With the police report in hand and a lot better perspective of the murder than I had when I walked into the precinct, I realized I had a big challenge ahead of me.

Driving back to the Hillcrest at this time of day, I knew I'd be dealing with commute traffic even though it was a reverse commute. I thought I'd better call the house and leave a message for Brad. "Hey, Brad, I'm on my way home and caught in traffic, and wanted to let you know I'll be late. It's been a really rough day and I can't wait to get home and tell you about it. I'll need a drink too, so have my tini glass on ice for me, Babe. Love ya . . . see you soon."

The slow drive home gave me time to process the information regarding the murder details that Chief Tallerico had just revealed to me. I was looking forward to getting home and being able to talk to Brad. He's my "rock" and could offer me the consolation I so desperately needed. I still couldn't believe that Gus was dead. He'd been such a special friend and such a kind man. Who could do something like this? Surely the murderer wasn't someone who knew him the way his friends did.

8

The Investigation

"Hey, Brad, I'm so happy to see you!" I hugged him tightly and didn't want to let him go.

"What is it, Tony? What's wrong?"

"It's been a really rough day and I have some bad news."

"Well, let me fix you a cosmo, while you go change your clothes and get comfortable."

"Thanks, Babe. . . . I love you!" I went to our bedroom to get changed, and while removing the contents from my pants pocket, I pulled out the check that Robert de Saint Cyr had given me as a retainer. This was the first time I'd looked at it and I was shocked to see the amount he was paying me to secure my services. It was obvious he was sincere about wanting to find the murderer.

"Brad, look at this." I showed him the check for ten thousand dollars.

"Tony, what is this for? Why is Robert giving you such a huge amount of money?"

"It's a sad story, Babe. He hired me to investigate

ah . . . situation. This is the retainer he paid me today."

"Wow. That seems like a pretty hefty sum, Tony. What's the investigation about?"

With cocktails now in hand, the two of us retired to the couch in the living room. I took a deep breath and began to tell Brad the whole story as I knew it. The details of Gustavo's murder sickened Brad as well.

"Oh, Tony . . . I'm so sorry. I know you've known Gus for a long time."

"Yes, and he's . . . was, such a good guy."

Puzzled by this, Brad said, "Why would anyone do something like this? It has to be a random act."

"Well, that's what I'm going to find out. Robert is paying me well, but I would take this on for free just to be able to bring the bastards to justice for what they've done."

We finished our drinks while we kicked around several ideas but nothing seemed to make sense.

"So, Hon, if you want to retreat to the guest bedroom office to get started on your investigation, I'll run down to the Chinese take-out on the corner and get a quick dinner for us. How does that sound?"

"Thanks, Brad. That would be great. I've got so many thoughts in my head now that I need to get down on paper. Also, I want to read over the police report and have a plan formulated by morning as to how I should begin to attack this investigation."

By the time we'd finished dinner I'd had time to

contemplate my notes and the police report, and was able to create an initial cohesive plan of action for the investigation. First I knew I had to obtain the guest list of those in attendance, as well as those who'd declined to attend the party, and run a background check on everyone. I really had my doubts that any of them could have done this, but I had to start somewhere.

Next, I needed to recall all that I saw the night of the party to see if anything seemed out of the ordinary. For me, the entire party was out of the ordinary, but nothing sinister immediately came to me.

I finally crawled into bed next to Brad about two o'clock in the morning but still was unable to sleep, thinking of any possible scenarios that I might be missing. While tossing and turning, suddenly a thought came to me.

I remembered the valet parking guy who'd had Gus cornered in the kitchen when I'd gone to say goodbye that night. That whole thing had felt a little menacing at that time and even more so now, thinking back on it. This character seemed like an aggressive hothead who might have come back later and killed Gus. I knew I had to find him and investigate him and his background to see if he had a possible motive. If he didn't have an alibi for after his work detail that night, he could be my prime suspect. I wish now that I'd mentioned to Brad the altercation that I'd witnessed that night when I found

Gus in the kitchen.

I didn't sleep much and when I got to my office the next morning, I called Mr. de Saint Cyr first thing.

"Morning, Robert."

The butler had answered the phone and passed the call on to Robert. "Yes ... a good morning to you, Mr. Tony."

"I wanted to run a few things by you. First off, if you have that list of the party guests for me, I was wondering if you could fax it to my office."

"I would be most happy to do that, Tony. The list I have here and I would be most happy to have someone fax it to you shortly. Can I assume your fax number is on the business card you offered me?"

"Yes, that would be great. ... I also need the names of your staff that were working that night. And your security that night—were they hired from a business or do they work for you?"

"I hire them to work for me but they work for others as well. They are not my employees. I will get you the names for the security on board that night if you like."

"That would be great. I recall there was some sort of altercation involving security when Brad and I arrived and I think I should question them about that."

"Sure, Tony, I understand your concern."

"Also ... the valet parking business that you hired? What was the name of that company?"

"I would not know this ... Gustavo would take care of

those details. He hires people and I pay . . . however, allow me to check with my accountant. It is quite possible the bill has been received. You know with these businesses, the bill is in the mail even before the affair."

"That would be great, Robert. As soon as you have a business name for me, let me know. I really want to follow up on a lead that I have concerning the valet parking staff."

"I check with my accountant today and let you know, Tony."

"Thanks. I think that's all I need right now. I'll be in touch and check back with you if I have more questions."

"Thanks. My pleasure to speak with you and I hope I have been of some help."

Later that day a fax came in with the names of all invited party guests as well as a list of the security guards working that night, with contact information for each.

I spent all the next day doing background checks and coming up with nothing. I called each of the four security guards and set up appointments to question them individually. I was really curious to find out more about the incident with the party crashers.

It was early Friday morning, nearly a week since the murder, and I was not any closer to figuring out what had happened. I'd only been working on the case less than 48 hours, but I was angry and overly anxious to find these bastards.

The memorial service for Gus was later that morning and Brad and I made plans to meet beforehand at about ten and head over to the mortuary chapel together. I expected a large crowd since Gus had a lot of friends and came from a large Hispanic family as well.

The chapel was filled with mourners with standing room only, and the sweet fragrance from the abundance of flowers in the room filled the air. The prayer-like sounds of Enya's music resonated as people sobbed with grief over the loss of such a young soul. It was a very moving tribute to my lost friend and helped me with closure. I was now faced with the commitment to myself and to Gus to find those responsible for his death.

My first appointment that afternoon after the memorial service was with one of the security guards, Bruno, followed by three more appointments later in the day with the other three guys.

Bruno was a big bruiser, the type you'd want as a security guard if you needed to be protected. There was nothing unusual about him except his walk. One leg was longer than the other and he wore a built up shoe, causing him to limp when he walked. Since Bruno was not directly involved with the altercation that took place on the pier, he really didn't have much information for me.

The next two interviews turned up nothing as well. They all indicated that Tommy, my last interview of the day, was the one who'd dealt with these party crashers.

"Hello, Tommy, nice to meet you." Tommy lived in a small tract home in a nice middle-income neighborhood. Several children were playing in the front yard when I approached his front door, and it appeared Tommy's was one of very few black families in this predominantly white neighborhood. I extended my hand to shake his as he opened the screen door. "I hope you don't mind me asking you a few questions about the night of Mr. de Saint Cyr's party."

"Not at all. I just hope I can help."

"I wanted to ask you specifically about the couple who tried to crash the party that you had to escort off the pier that night."

"Yeah, they were pretty argumentative that night and were obviously not invited guests by the way they were dressed. I could smell alcohol on the breath of the gentleman ... if I could call him that."

"Did they try to tell you they were 'invited' guests?"

"They didn't really try to say they were invited. The guy just kept saying he had a right to be there and kept asking to speak to Robert. He began to get physical with me and that was when I called for backup from the other guys."

"So you had asked them to leave but they refused and you had to physically remove them from the pier?"

"Yeah, pretty much. The whole thing took maybe ten minutes but was enough to create a scene and that agitated Mr. de Saint Cyr."

"Did Mr. de Saint Cyr know this guy or did he get a look at him?"

"No, we kept Robert down below in the Master Suite of the ship to avoid possible harm. This guy seemed pretty wacked out. We weren't sure what he might do. We tried to calm them down as we escorted them off the pier."

"Did he at any time pull a weapon on you . . . a gun or knife?"

"No, he actually seemed pretty harmless, just more of a heckler and the party-crasher type of person."

"And . . . the woman trying to board the yacht with him? How was she acting?"

"She was pretty quiet . . . but yes, she was with him and trying to force her way on-board also."

"At any time did you ever get a name for either of them?"

"No. As I said, they never claimed that their name was on the guest list, only that they had a right to be there, but they never said what that meant."

"All right, thanks, Tommy. This is helpful."

"Oh yeah . . . one more thing, Tony. Now that I think of it, I do recall the woman saying a couple of times when

I was escorting them off the pier, she said, 'c'mon Jackie, let's just go.'"

"Thanks. That's helpful. If you think of anything else, please give me a call. Here's my card. I appreciate all your help."

"No problem, I hope you catch the murderer."

I stopped off at SD Koffi Grinders on my way back to my office for an iced mocha and to make more detailed notes from my four interviews. Checking my phone messages, I saw I had a call from Robert.

"Hallo Tony, this is Robert. ... I check with my accountant, the bill for valet service was delivered yesterday. The name is ... um, hold on, let me get it here ... it is 'Elite Limo and Party Services.' I hope this will be of help to you. I would expect they have a computer site with their phone and address, but if you need help with that, you call me. Good luck, Tony."

I googled my phone for a web site for Elite Limo in San Diego and found it. It was located across town, out by the pier. I knew I wanted to make a surprise visit to Elite Limo but the afternoon was already pretty shot. I planned to stop by the police station and talk with Chief Tallerico again on my way home ... that is, if he was still there this late on a Friday afternoon. My visit to Elite

Limo would have to wait until Saturday.

"Well, Chief ... surprised to find you still working this late on a Friday!"

"Come in, Mr. Felice. Unlike you, I am a public servant and I am accountable to the people of San Diego County. What can I do for you today?"

"I just wanted to check with you on the investigation, if you have any new evidence or leads?"

"Nothing yet that I can share with you, Mr. Felice. ... And do you have anything new?"

"I'm working on a few things but nothing to speak of. ... This may seem like an odd request to you. The police report states that the cause of death was from 'blunt force trauma to the right frontal cranial.' If I recall, you indicated you were not sure if the blow on the head killed Gus or if he died hitting his head when he landed on the marble floor after being struck."

Chief Tallerico responded, "You can speculate and argue either point. The autopsy was inconclusive as to that point. What does that matter anyway?"

"Well, I guess it doesn't matter now but it could have a lot of bearing in a court trial to the jury. It could mean the difference between premeditated murder or involuntary manslaughter. I was wondering if I could I have a look at the murder weapon ... or should I say the assault object."

"I don't know what purpose that would serve, but I have

no problems with that. I can have one of my men escort you to the evidence room. You realize you will not be able to handle any of the evidence without wearing gloves."

"I know the routine, Chief. I'm not new to this business."

"Very good then. If there's nothing else, let me get someone to take you to the evidence room."

"Thanks, Chief."

The object used to assault Gus was the only bit of evidence I was interested in. This was probably more for my own curiosity than anything else. I put on the rubber gloves and removed the trophy piece used in the assault from the plastic bag. It was indeed an Oscar, and it had been awarded for Best Director to Robert de Saint Cyr for his last movie, *Still Waters Run Deep*. How ironic was that.

❧

The entire week had me consumed with this investigation. Brad had never been around me when I get caught up with an assignment like this. Being personally involved in this case gave me even more motivation to solve it, and I was starting to feel vibes that he was getting a little irritated with me.

"Brad, remember the night of the party while we were waiting in line to board the yacht? Remember the couple who tried to crash the party that night?"

"Yeah ... I remember we had to wait while they were

escorted off the pier."

"I just wish I could find them to question them more about their motive that night and why they felt they should be at that party. It's a little weird to me."

"It does sound a little coincidental to me too."

"Another thing, Brad, that I never told you happened that night."

"Oh gawd, now what?"

"Well, when we got ready to leave and I stepped into the kitchen galley to say goodbye to Gus, he was arguing with one of the valet parking attendants."

"That's a little strange but maybe it had something to do with Gus's car ... or maybe they were friends. You don't know."

"No, this was more of a threatening conversation ... had me a little worried and I wish I'd mentioned it to you that night."

"Whatever. ... You know, Tony, you need to take a break. You're running yourself down with this obsession. How about tomorrow I take you to brunch at Moe's and then we run out to the beach for the day and just relax ... take a day off."

"Thanks, Babe, but I can't. Tomorrow I need to talk to the valet parking service and see if I can locate that guy who argued with Gus. Plus, I have a million other things I need to follow up on and notes to make and update."

"Fine! ... Just trying to help. ... You know, come to

think of it, I have some tests to grade and some other school work to get caught up on as well, so I think I'm going to spend the night at my apartment and spend the day tomorrow getting caught up."

"Oh, c'mon, Babe, don't be mad."

"I'm not mad ... just need some space ... and you probably need to be left alone to do your thing for a while."

"What I need is your support. I know you've never seen me like this when I'm so focused on a case. I'm sorry you feel that my 'obsession' is more than you can deal with right now."

"Hey, no problem, I just need to take some time away, ... away from it all. And as I say, I have plenty of school work that I need to get caught up on anyway. If I spend the weekend at my apartment near campus, I can get more done."

I was shocked to hear Brad be so negative about my commitment to my work. I thought he already knew what being married to a detective was like. Apparently I was wrong.

This was the first time that Brad and I had had a disagreement since he moved in and the first night we'd spend apart because of it. I was very conflicted and heartbroken over this, but I needed to keep my focus on the job that I was hired to do. I could only hope that Brad would come to understand the nature of my career and the commitment that is required of a Private Investigator when on assignment to solve a case—especially one such as this, the murder of a friend. If our relationship could survive this test, we could likely make it through anything.

Brad packed a small overnight bag and some of his school work and with a gentle kiss on the cheek and a goodbye, walked out. . . . Would I see him again?

9

The Suspect

I didn't sleep well at all without Brad lying next to me. When I woke up Saturday morning, not only was my mind filled with scenarios of the investigation, I was also concerned for our relationship. Could we survive this disagreement and come to a meeting of the minds? Time would tell, but right then I knew I needed to let Brad have some time to himself. I just hoped to hear from him by the end of the day. Hopefully he wasn't going to spend the entire weekend at his apartment. And if I didn't hear from him, should I try calling him, or should I just leave him alone until he was ready?

I set out to follow my lead on the valet parking attendant at Elite Limo. Driving across town to the office location of the business, I couldn't help notice the seedy part of town in which it was located. The address I had took me to a large warehouse building that housed a garage shop where the limos were parked, as well as their business office.

The metal door was slightly ajar, and I pushed it open. The garage smelled of oil and was dark inside. "Good morning! . . . Anyone around?" I yelled out.

"Yo, mornin. . . . Howudoin?" The greeting came from a small interior office. I stuck my head inside to find a desk with piles of dog-eared paperwork, empty cans and bottles everywhere, and an abundance of female pin-up photos adorning the walls.

The small office reeked with cigarette smoke. "Is the business owner around?" A short, stocky, very Italian looking guy sat behind the desk with his feet up, watching a small black and white television set. He had on a grimy tee shirt, with dark hair creeping out the front and back of the neckline, and had a very thin patch of greasy hair on the top of his head. . . . Surely HE was not the owner.

"Nah . . . Joe's nevah heah. Sumin I can help yous wit?"

"Well, I hope so. I attended a party recently with valet parking attendants and I was hoping to locate one of the guys working that night and talk with him."

"So, whos waz zit? . . . Yous gotta name?"

"I don't have a name, just a description. He's about 5' 10" and Hispanic looking. He had a tattoo on his forearm of a circle with black and white ink. . . . Does that sound familiar?" I knew not to bother identifying the tattoo as a yin-yang symbol with this character.

He was already nodding his head when I mentioned

the tattoo, as if he knew right away who I was talking about. "Yous mean Roody. Yeah, heeze heah. Heeze out back washin a kar. Follow me."

We headed across the floor to a back exit. I tried to avoid the grease spots on the concrete as we walked past several shiny black limos. "Yeah ... sum kidz rented da limo for der twenty-frst brday prty last week an the damn kidz coudn't hold da liquor ... puked all over the friggin kar ... nside an out. Hellova mess. Damn kidz. ... Yo Roody? Dis guy wantsta tawk ta yous."

"Thanks. ... Hi, Rudy. I was at a party you worked last weekend and I'd like to ask you a couple of questions, if you wouldn't mind."

"Okay. ... Yeah, I worked a party on Saturday and one on Friday too."

"Well, this was Saturday evening, the yacht party for Robert de Saint Cyr."

"Oh yeah, great gig ... made some good money that night. What can I do for you? ... Your car wasn't damaged, was it?"

"No, everything was fine. I was the guy who walked in on you in the kitchen when you were arguing with Gus."

"Oh yeah, I thought you looked familiar. You weren't supposed to see that."

"I had a hunch I walked in at the wrong time. So what was the argument about?"

"Who wants to know? I think that's between us, and

you need to talk to Gus if you want to find out and he ain't gonna say anything either."

"Well, that's why I'm here. My name is Tony Felice and I'm a private investigator hired by Mr. de Saint Cyr."

"So what is it that you want with me?"

"You don't know, do you?"

"Know what?"

"Gus was murdered that night on the yacht, and you're shaping up to be my number one suspect."

"No shit? God damn!" His seemingly happy demeanor suddenly changed. He looked visibly shaken at the thought of Gus having been murdered. He asked, "So why do you think I had anything to do with it?"

"Because I witnessed you and him arguing over something, and I want to know what that was. And I want to know what you were doing that evening after the party ended."

"I wouldn't kill him."

"Then talk to me. Tell me what was going on that night."

"I can't tell you."

"Listen, you better start talking or you'll remain the number one suspect and I'll make sure the police know all about what I saw that night in the kitchen."

"Oh geeze. You gotta promise me you won't tell my wife. I gotta kid and a wife . . . I don't wanna lose that."

"We'll see about that. Let's start from the beginning. How is it that you knew Gus?"

"Oh geeze." He kept rubbing his forehead and shaking his bowed head. He seemed very nervous and uncomfortable. "I met Gus at an AA meeting about a year or so ago. He had just moved here."

"Are you still going to your AA meetings?"

"Yes. . . . When I met him I thought he was a pretty hot guy."

"Okay ... how is that?"

"Geeze, don't let my wife know about this. I've been married for about ten years now and I've got a little boy, but sometimes ..."

"Yeah, go ahead. . . . You need to tell me and I'll keep it to myself if I possibly can. What is it?"

"Okay, I'm married, you know, but sometimes ... sometimes I like to be with a guy. . . . I like to take it up the ass, okay?"

I was not expecting that but I tried not to show my astonishment by this confession since I could relate to what he was saying. It just came as a bit of a shock from this butch-type guy. "So did you and Gus ever connect? Were you having an affair or something?"

"No. I knew he was gay and I could see that big basket he had and I wanted to take that up my ass, but he would never do it. He said he wouldn't cheat with me on my wife."

"So was that what you were arguing about that night of the party?"

"Yeah. . . . I wanted him to take me home after work and thought we could have a quick fuck before we left the yacht."

"And he wouldn't go for it?"

"No, I couldn't convince him."

"So what time did you leave the yacht that night and how did you get home?"

"My wife had the car and I rode to work that night with my bud Steve. He gave me a ride home and I guess we left about two in the morning."

"And where did you go when the two of you left?"

"Steve took me home and dropped me off."

"Can your wife verify that story?"

"Yes, but I don't want her to know."

"I won't have to say anything about your sexual fantasies, but I need to verify your whereabouts later that night. I'll need to talk to Steve too and get his story."

"My wife woke up and talked to me briefly when I got home and then went back to sleep. . . . Just don't say anything about the sex stuff, please, man."

"I will certainly do what I can to not let that become an issue."

"And . . . don't tell the police, please."

"Why is that Rudy?"

"I just got off probation a while back and that wouldn't be good for me if they found out I was being investigated in conjunction with a murder. They'd nail me."

"You're right, Rudy. That doesn't sound good."

"But, I've been clean for over ten years now ... since I've been married, and since I quit drinking."

"Well ... that's good news but it still wouldn't look good for you."

"I could never hurt Gus. I liked the kid. You gotta believe me."

"Well, I want to confirm your whereabouts later that evening but I appreciate the information. I'll do what I can to keep the police from knowing this if I think you're telling me the truth and I can verify your story."

"Thanks."

"One more thing. ... Can I get your address so I can stop by and talk to your wife? ... And when is the best time to talk to Steve? I need to get a phone number for him?"

He gave me Steve's cell phone number and his wife's name and their home address. He then again begged me not to tell his wife of his sexual escapades. I took advantage of the moment to remind him that since he is cheating on his wife he might want to play safe and use a condom at ALL times so as not to bring home any STDs and especially AIDS to his unsuspecting wife.

On my way home I stopped by to see Rudy's wife. I wanted to talk to her before he got home. I didn't need to tell her anything of his sexual fantasies about Gus, but I was able to confirm that Rudy was home and in bed shortly after two in the morning. His story checked out with his wife.

Then I stopped by my office even though it was closed. I went in to call Steve and check out Rudy's story about getting a ride with him that night after their work detail. Steve verified that Rudy had hitched a ride with him both to work and home afterward. He said Rudy told him his wife had the car. He verified that he dropped Rudy off at his house about ten after two in the morning, after working the party that night.

Since I had Rudy's name and home address, I decided to run a background check and see what the probation was for. I was a little shocked at what I found, but as he had said, all of this was in the past—at least ten years ago or more. Seems he has a pretty good sized rap sheet from when he was a young stud. Aggravated assault, breaking and entering, drunk driving, resisting arrest … he was hardly a choir boy by any means. However, I tended to think he was telling me the truth, and that his marriage and son had helped him turn his life around. I'm sure being clean and sober also helped him clean up his act.

❧

By early afternoon, I had still heard nothing from Brad. I thought about calling him but decided I'd wait until I got home and maybe he would be there waiting for me. If not, I could call him that evening. I decided to get up from my desk for a cup of coffee and shake the Brad concerns from my head and get back on the investigation.

I felt a little bit frustrated having exhausted my one viable lead for Gus's murder. Where to go from here? The thought of the party crashers kept returning to me. With no way of locating them to question their story, I had nowhere to turn. Maybe some of the guests who were in the area at the time of the altercation might have heard something. This of course would mean tracking down dozens more people to find out what they might know.

Driving home from my office, my head was a maze of thoughts with nothing really making sense and the maze leading to a dead end. I took the freeway exit that heads into the Hillcrest as I had done so many times, before making the stop for the light. The homeless tended to hang out at this corner, and today was no exception. A homeless man with a piece of cardboard that read *"will work for money"* was standing next to the corner.

What was different for me this time was that I flashed on the homeless man sleeping on the pier that night of the party. He had seemed to be somewhat of a fixture at that warm safe location on the pier, and just maybe he might have some information to help me locate the murderer or at least locate the party crashers. I hoped that if I returned at night to that location again I could find him. And, possibly with a few bucks in hand, I could buy some information from him that would help me.

Walking into the condo, I realized that Brad had not come back, and that saddened me. Should I call him? ... I noticed the phone message light blinking on the land line—but surely Brad wouldn't call and leave a message there for me unless ... he really didn't want to talk to me. Hitting the retrieve-messages button, I saw I had three calls and one of those was a forwarded call from my office. On weekends I usually have all my business calls forwarded to my home phone.

The first call was a political recorded message from Martin Sheen. Yeah, right. The second was a hang-up. The third call had been forwarded from my office at around one o'clock.

"Beep! ... *Third message delivered from remote number, sent at 1:14 p.m. today.*" "*Hey ... Mr. Felice. This is Chief Tallerico. I just wanted to tell you that you can drop your investigation. We've found our man. I'm sending our guys out to his house to bring him in soon. His fingerprints were found all over the yacht and he has a long criminal record. His name is Rudy Garcia. Just wanted to let you know.*"

Shit! This was not good news. I needed to talk to the Chief and let him know what I'd already learned about Rudy and that I believed he had nothing to do with the murder. From my previous experience with the police department, I feared they'd be blinded by any other information and ready to pin this case on someone and close it out. A quickly solved murder case makes them look good. They surely don't want to be left with an unsolved murder. And this certainly wouldn't fare too well for Rudy being able to keep his secret from his wife.

Mentally and physically exhausted, I lay down to take a bit of a break and fell fast asleep.

10

Communication Skills

I slept for two hours and at five o'clock I was awakened by the sound of rattling keys and the front door opening. It was Brad ... at least I assumed it was Brad—and that brought a smile to my face. He came back! Without bothering to smooth out the hair bumps from my nap, I ran to the living room to greet him.

"Hey, Babe, I missed you last night." I hugged him tightly.

His strong sexy arms around me, I could feel the warmth of his body through his shirt, and his breath on my ear as he whispered, "Yeah, I didn't sleep all that well either thinking about you. I'm sorry I wasn't more understanding. That was pretty selfish of me, but I just tripped out. I'm sorry, Hon."

I leaned back, looking up at him into those puppy-dog eyes that made me crazy. "Sometimes that happens and it's okay. It's just something we need to work on. I know I'm guilty of being too consumed with my work."

"But that's who you are, and I need to understand that

and be supportive. I'm just not used to seeing this kind of intense dedication, being a teacher ... the students I work with are not of that mind set—God knows I wish they were more so." Brad pulled me into him once again with a big bear hug.

"And ... I want us to be able to talk to each other when we have things on our mind that concern us," I said. "The best relationships are those that communicate, so please tell me when I'm doing something that upsets you and let's talk about it. Okay?" I was feeling my eyes well up with tears as I became more emotional.

"Deal!" he said. "I want to know more about your work and I want to get involved if I can so it's more interesting for me as well. I could tell you more about my teaching at the University, but I don't think you would find that very fascinating."

"Sure it would be. I'm interested in anything you do and want to be a part of your life and help you through the tough times, and share in the good times."

"Not too many fun times in teaching ... but then there aren't a lot of tough times either. It's actually a pretty boring career, unlike that of a high profile private investigator. What is it that they call you again ... the Naked Dick?"

"And I wear that title proudly."

"Well, Hon, I don't want to spend another night without you by my side."

"Me neither, Babe."

"Can I treat you to dinner out tonight … maybe Baja Betty's?"

I'd thought of trying to get to the pier tonight to see if I could track down the homeless man we'd encountered the night of the party, and see if I could get anything from him that would help me with the investigation. But after Brad's homecoming and invitation for dinner I didn't dare put a damper on things since it seemed to be going so well. Maybe I could involve him in checking out the pier tomorrow evening. "Dinner sounds great, Brad. I need to make a quick phone call to the Police Chief and then I'll get ready."

"What time do you want to go?"

"Maybe in a couple of hours, like around seven or 7:30?"

"That would be great. I love you, Tony."

"Love you, Brad, and welcome home."

I knew I needed to get in touch with Chief Tallerico to convince him to back off of Rudy as his number one suspect in the murder investigation.

I didn't expect to find him at the police station on a Saturday afternoon but maybe I could leave him a message.

I got through to the receptionist. "Good afternoon, Mr. Felice. Chief Tallerico isn't in but I can put you through to his voice mail if you like."

"Thank you . . . that would be great."

"Good afternoon, Chief. This is Tony Felice. I received your message and I wanted to get back to you. . . . I've already spoken to Rudy and he is NOT your man. His alibi checks out and he is clean. He's turned his life around and there's a good reason for his fingerprints being in the galley aboard the yacht. Do what you have to do, but don't rush to judgment on Rudy. Wait until I have a chance to talk to you. I'll plan to come in and see you first thing on Monday. Give me a call if anything else comes up . . . but again please, don't assume your killer is Rudy. There's much more to it than meets the eye. Thanks, I'll be talking to you soon."

When Brad and I got to Baja Betty's it was busy as usual. Before putting our name on the list and being assigned one of those vibrating pocket reservation thingy's, we noticed Carlo and Sam at the bar and made our way over to them. They were dining alone and asked us to join them, so our wait for a table was shortened. Besides, we hadn't seen the two of them since that night aboard the yacht, and maybe they'd seen or heard something that might be helpful to me. I thought of this as sort of an informal interview with many more guests still to be questioned.

We were shown to our table. With drinks on the way from the bar, Carlo was dying to ask me about the case. "So Tony, what's happening with the murder investigation? I was so shocked when Robert de Saint Cyr called me to get information in order to contact you."

"That came as a huge shock to me as well. I've known Gus for about 15 years, I guess. Currently I'm still trying to get a good lead on a possible murder suspect. Any ideas?"

"Yeah, right … I wish I had something for you. If I were a psychic, I wouldn't be selling my paintings; I'd be giving them away since I'd already be rich."

"I just can't seem to get a lead. It's frustrating."

Sounding very confused and frustrated himself, Carlo said, "I've been thinking over and over about that evening and I can't think of anything unusual that I observed. It almost seems like the murder was not even connected with the party and was just a random act."

"Well, I would hope that's true, as I'd hate to think that any of Robert's guests or employees would have anything to do with this murder. But … I can't rule out anyone or any possible scenario in the course of my investigation."

I was beginning to worry that all this talk about my work and the investigation might be once again upsetting Brad. I guess I was wrong as he seemed to be more interested than I was giving him credit for. "Hon, the only thing that I thought was a little peculiar that evening was the scuffle on the pier when we arrived, but we never did find out what that was about, did we?"

"Not really, Brad, but funny you should bring that up,

as that's a lead I'm trying to follow up on."

Sam said, "Yeah, Carlo and I observed some of that from the deck of the yacht. All we heard was that they were a couple of party crashers. You could tell they weren't invited guests by the way they were dressed. Not sure who they thought they were fooling."

"That's just it, Sam. They weren't trying to fool anyone—all they kept saying is that they had a right to be there. Very strange!"

I decided it would be best if we let this conversation go, as we were getting nowhere with this. "So guys, I'm starving, should we order?"

"Good idea, Tony." Carlo spoke up, "Now that I have my '*prickly pear cactus margarita*,' I'm good."

We had a nice relaxing dinner with good friends, and it was nice to be going home with Brad to share my bed and lounge around in the morning. I try not to work on Sundays if I can possibly avoid it, and especially this Sunday it seemed more important for Brad and me to spend time together. I'd be busy on the investigation again on Monday morning. I looked forward to sharing more with Brad, now that we'd brought some clarity to what we wanted from each other in our relationship. "*. . . Maybe this time, things will be different . . . Maybe this time I'll win. . .*"

Our Sunday was spent relaxing at Black's Beach with a little picnic lunch and a bottle of wine. Brad was finally comfortable enough to shed his board shorts and get naked with the rest of the beach goers. Once he'd gotten used to it, he was able to enjoy the feeling of being free of textiles and of running naked on the beach in the sand. And I felt very proud that this sexy naked man was my husband. Surely I was the envy of all the men on the beach that day since that hot man was with *me*.

∽

Monday morning just after 7:00 a.m. I was awakened by my phone ringing.

"Morning, Mr. Felice. I hope I didn't wake you."

"Oh ... yeah. Good morning, Chief Tallerico. No, that's all right. I was getting up soon."

"Good. I wanted to get back to you after getting your message from Saturday. If you have something I should know about, I'd like to talk to you, but I think we're about to close this case."

Damn it! I was afraid of this. "No, no, you don't have the murderer yet. .... Rudy is not your guy."

"Well, as I said, I welcome any new information you might have but my men will be picking Rudy up later today for questioning and possibly booking him."

"Let me just come in and talk to you, Chief, before you jump to conclusions."

"Fine. Why don't you stop by my office this morning

around ten and let me know what's on your mind. This better be good because we've got a lot of evidence against this guy."

"Sounds great, Chief. I'll see you then."

Brad was just getting out of the shower. I had a pot of coffee on and was gathering some of my paperwork together along with my notebook and favorite Cross pen. After a quick shower myself, I decided to stop in at work before going to the police station.

"Brad, I'm headed in to the office and I have a ten o'clock appointment this morning."

"I need to get going, too, and get to school. I'm running late."

"I made a fresh pot of coffee, Brad."

"Thanks, Hon, but I'm just going to run through the drive-through at SD Koffi on my way. I really need a mocha this morning."

"No problem. ... Hey, Brad, do you want to go with me this evening to check out a lead that I have on this case?" I was a little nervous about asking but I wanted to include Brad. And I felt I could use the support, and thought this would be a great opportunity for him to see what I do for a living.

Trying to sound very mysterious, Brad said, "This sounds like a dangerous mission. Not sure I want you going alone, so count me in."

"Really? Great. I can fill you in with more of the

details after you get home from work. We won't be going out until late in the evening to pursue the lead that I have, and I hope it gets me somewhere."

With a kiss goodbye, Brad was out the door and I was not far behind him. I had my traveler mug filled with coffee and I was off to the office to check my messages and gather my thoughts for my meeting with Chief Tallerico.

∾

"Good morning, Mr. Felice. Chief Tallerico is expecting you. You can go on back … you know where his office is?"

"Yes, thank you."

"Morning, Mr. Felice." The Chief met me at his office door with a handshake. It seemed that after our rocky start, Chief Tallerico and I now had a meeting of the minds and a slowly growing respect for one another.

"Morning, Chief. Glad you're taking the time to hear what I have to say. I think you'll find the time worth your while and will save some possible embarrassment on your part."

I could see that last comment did not sit well with Chief Tallerico, being a proud man, but I meant it in the best possible way and not as a dig.

"First, let me tell you that I know for a fact that Rudy was aboard the yacht, because I saw him in the galley the night of the party. Naturally you would have found his fingerprints on the yacht."

"You have my curiosity aroused, so go on."

"Let me ask you, Chief, did you find Rudy's prints on the murder weapon or on the dingy get-away boat?"

"Well . . . no. Those prints lifted didn't match Rudy's."

"Exactly—and that's because he didn't kill Gus."

"But he has a criminal history, so he's the most logical suspect and we've got his fingerprints at the scene of the crime."

"I thought that same thing, but just hear me out. First off, the criminal history you speak of is all in the past, ten years ago or more. Rudy no longer drinks and after getting married and being clean and sober, he's changed his life around. His family means the world to him."

"How is it that you know all this stuff, Mr. Felice?"

"Don't forget I'm a Private Investigator—this is what I do for a living, Chief."

"So this still doesn't explain why Rudy's prints were found on the yacht."

"Well, let me tell you. I'm guessing I can pinpoint for you exactly where the prints were found on the yacht. . . . All his prints found were in the galley, correct?"

"The ones we could find and read . . . yes, they were all in the galley of the yacht."

"The night of the party, just before heading home, I walked into the galley to say goodbye to Gus, who was a longtime friend of mine. I didn't see Gus at first but I could hear his voice and that of another man arguing—it seemed to be coming from around the corner near the walk-in box."

"That's where Rudy's prints were found."

"Yes, and I felt like Gus might be in trouble so I confronted the man and he left abruptly."

"So, that just gives Rudy even more motive to have killed Gus if they were fighting over something. I don't think I understand."

"Well, that's what I thought too, so I tracked down Rudy and questioned him. His alibi checked out. After work, he rode home with a co-worker who dropped him off at his house. I then checked with his wife who verified the time he got home and that he went right to bed with her. His story checks out."

"I don't know. It's still a little suspicious to me. I'm going to want to question him further myself. What was the fight about? Did you find that out too?"

"I did and this part might be a little hard for you to understand, but is perfectly believable to me, being a gay man."

Chief Tallerico seemed to squirm a little in his chair after my last comment but he was listening intently.

"Let me try to explain this to you without being too blatant or graphic. Rudy first met Gus about a year ago at an AA meeting and liked him. He'd tried a couple of times in the past to get Gus to sleep with him."

"Wait, wait . . . wait. This guy Rudy is married with a kid."

"Right, he is and that's why he wants to keep this part of his life private. Especially from his wife. He likes to have sex with men on occasion."

Now seemingly very confused, the Chief said, "I don't understand that."

"I thought you might have problems with this, Chief, but try to be open minded. This sort of thing is not at all uncommon."

With a sigh he responded, "All right . . . go on."

"Well, Gus would never have sex with Rudy because he didn't want to be a part of Rudy cheating on his wife, and Rudy was frustrated with that. Since he was working the yacht party that night, he tried again to coerce Gus into having sex with him and Gus refused again. That's what the argument was about and Rudy left once I walked in on them. Rudy had no idea that Gus was murdered later that night while Rudy was home in bed sleeping."

The Chief was now scratching his head with confusion. "Geeze . . . what a mess! How in the hell . . ."

"Rudy is very concerned that his wife doesn't find out about his sexual escapades since he loves her and adores his kid. He has turned his life around. He just had this quirky sexual fantasy about Gus, but I think many of us are guilty of our fantasies—right, Chief?"

"Nothing like *that*."

"But still … we all have our fantasies. Can you possibly be sensitive to his secret and keep his wife from finding out?"

"I don't know, Tony. I'll have to question him about this and see if his story checks out with what you've told me. If I possibly can keep his wife from finding out about this sexual thing that he has going, I will, but I'm making no promises. That's not my problem here."

"Thanks, Chief. That's all I can ask of you. I think you'll find as I did that Rudy is innocent and had nothing to do with the murder of Gus."

"I'll check it out and I'll get back with you. I appreciate this information."

We shook hands again as a sign of our partnership commitment to solving this murder case together. I left his office feeling pretty good about my investigation skills. I hoped those skills would be working well for me later that evening when Brad and I attempted to locate the homeless man on the pier and try to gather some credible information thru him.

11

Possible Witness

When Brad got home from work, I met him at the door with a mandarin cosmo. The two of us adjourned to the patio with our drinks to discuss the mission I had in mind for us later that evening. Brad appeared to be excited about my plan and felt it was a good idea to follow up with the homeless man we'd seen on the pier the night of the party. It was very likely this might be the only eyewitness as to what occurred that night of Gus's murder.

After hearing my plan, Brad got up and went to our kitchen pantry. He returned with a couple of bottles of "Two Buck Chuck" from Trader Joe's.

"If we expect to get any information from a wino, we need something to entice him. A bottle of cheap red should help." He smiled and gave me a look of exhilaration at the thought of our undertaking.

"Great idea, Babe. I hadn't thought of that. I did stop by the ATM to get a few twenties. I think we're pretty set with incentives to exchange for information."

We waited until nearly ten o'clock before leaving the house and took my car to the pier. I was nervous about the operation for some reason, but Brad appeared to be calm. I was glad he was there.

The parking lot was eerily deserted and dark, with only an occasional light pole. Several lights had been broken out, probably from target practice by young teens, while others were merely burned out, leaving weird and spooky shadows on the pier. We parked as near to the docks as we could and exited the car after a deep breath.

"Well, here goes nothing," I sighed.

"Think positive, Hon. This could be the break in the case you've been looking for."

As we walked along the wooden pier, with the sound of the waves lapping against the docked boats and the smell of creosote wood, I felt my heart beating faster. In the distance we could see the ice machine where we'd encountered the homeless man the night we boarded Robert's yacht. This time, however, it appeared the man was not there.

We kept walking even though I was beginning to feel disappointment that my mission appeared to be failing. Then to my surprise, as we approached the ice machine we noticed a pair of feet around the opposite side of the machine. This area of the deck was more protected from the sea breeze and still emitted warmth from the compressor motor.

"Look, Brad ... someone's there on the opposite side. Let's hope that is the same guy."

"Most likely it is, as these homeless guys are pretty territorial and stake claim to their 'home.'"

"Do you think we'll recognize him again, Brad?"

"I don't know. I guess we'll just see what we can find out and hope that it will be useful."

As we walked up to the old man, he appeared to be sleeping and I was hesitant to startle him. Not a good idea to get him irritated right off.

"Hello ... hello there ... how are you this evening? Keeping warm enough?" Stupid question, I realized after I said it.

The old man began to squirm from under his dirty tattered blanket. Two eyes peered at us from beneath a frayed knit cap. ... But there was no response.

I tried again. "Hello. What's your name?"

The old man just glared at me, clearly not happy that we were intruding. "Hi, I'm Tony and this is Brad. Could you use a little drink?"

I pulled out the twist top bottle of red wine and showed it to the man. His eyes appeared to light up. We'd finally gotten his attention and he started to pull himself up in a sitting position, all the time with his eyes fixed on the bottle.

"And your name is?"

He still appeared to be waking up but started to

mumble something. Finally, we heard him say "Frank. Everyone calls me Frank."

"Well, Frank, nice to meet you. Do you usually hang out here on the peer near the warmth of this machine?" I handed him the bottle of red wine.

The incentive Brad had suggested seemed to be working like a charm. The old man had decided to become talkative. "This is my home. You're not here to kick me out, are you?"

"No, no. Absolutely not. I'm just glad you have a place to call home and that you're comfortable with the warmth from this motor."

The old man removed the cap from the bottle and took a swig of wine. It was like medication to him and he sighed with comfort at the taste. "So, what do you guys want from me?" He asked.

"We just have a few questions to ask of you." I found a place to sit myself down on the pier not far from him. Brad was quick to follow. We both soon discovered the stench of body odor was something we would have to get used to.

"Do you remember a while back when there was a big party one evening that took place on a luxury yacht here?"

"Yeah ... whatever happened to that boat ... it was always right here next to me. I miss it. Did it sink?"

"No, Frank, it didn't sink. It's just being docked elsewhere for a while. It will be back soon." I wanted to keep him calm and not say much about the investigation at this point. I thought it best that I not take notes too, as this could make Frank uncomfortable.

"I'm glad, because that boat is like part of my furniture in my house here. Maybe sounds silly to you, but this is my home."

"I totally understand, Frank. . . . So do you recall that night of the party?"

"There are always a lot of parties on that boat, but I remember this was one of the big, fancy shmancy parties, you know. Men in penguin suits and all."

"Sounds like a fun time."

"Yeah, I guess if you're into that stuff. Seems like a waste in my opinion. But I did make some money that night. People were pretty nice to me."

"That's great, Frank. That's nice to hear. Do you recall any fights or disagreements that night?"

"Fights?" Frank looked up at me puzzled.

"Yeah, you know, any scuffles or disagreements among the guests?"

"Not really, not that I recall."

I knew that the squabble had taken place within a few feet of where we were sitting, but I wanted to verify this man's credibility to see just what he did remember. "So there was nothing that happened that might have involved the police or the security guards?"

"Oh yeah, that. Some of the guests, a man and

woman I believe, were forced off the pier by the guards. Not sure what that was about. Maybe they tried to steal something, I don't know. ... Say, what is all this about anyway? Why so many questions?" He took another swig of his wine.

"Well, Frank, we're trying to determine who might have been involved in a crime that took place that night and maybe you might know something that will be helpful to us."

"I didn't do anything. I didn't commit any crime."

"No, Frank, we know you're a good man, but you may have seen something that could be helpful to us." I decided this might be a good time to pull out a twenty dollar bill and refresh his memory a bit more.

"Here you go, Frank. I think anything you could help us with is worth paying for." I handed him the twenty and he reluctantly took it from my hand.

"Can I buy cigs with this?"

"Frank, you can use it for whatever you want ... it's your money. Now ... what do you recall about the couple that was ushered off the pier that night? Anything they might have said or done that may have been a little out of the ordinary? Did you hear either of them referred to by name?"

Frank was rolling his twenty in his hand playing with it like a new toy. "Nah, there was too much commotion at that time for me to hear anything, but later when they came back, I did talk to them—and I think I can remember their names, if I think about it."

Stunned, I looked at Brad, who appeared to be as thrilled as was I. I tried not to act too surprised, however. "So Frank ... you saw the two of them again later that evening?"

"Yeah, but it was three of them then. I think it was the same two from earlier and some other broad."

"And do you recall what time this was?"

"Sure, I remember looking at the grandfather clock in the hall." he said sarcastically. "Hell, I don't know what time it was. I don't own a watch ... it was late."

"So it was obviously after the party. Was the yacht ... err boat, here at that time?"

"Yeah, it had been back for maybe a couple of hours or so. I don't really know."

This was some really good stuff we were getting from Frank, and I was hoping he didn't shut down on us. Just to be sure, I pulled out the second bottle of wine and set it next to Brad, right in Frank's line of sight. "So, what did the man and two women do while on the pier with you?"

"We talked for a while. The floozy-looking broad gave me a cig and it was like I had died and gone to heaven. You know how long it's been since I had a smoke?"

"I'm sure it was, Frank. That was nice of her. Do you think you would recognize her again if you saw her?"

"Probably not ... it was a little dark, ya know."

"Do you recall any names of the three people you talked with?"

"Only one I can think of now is the guy ... the one gal called him Jack. I remember that because I had a big red tabby cat as a kid that was named Jack and this guy had red hair too."

That name was consistent with what we'd been told by security. The only confusion in my mind was the third person, the other woman, the floozy, as Frank put it. "Can you describe any of these three people, Frank?"

"I don't think so ... it was dark, like I said. One thing I do recall about the woman that lighted my cig ... when she put her hand down with the lit match, I noticed she had a small rose tattoo on the back of her hand—between her thumb and index finger."

"Do you recall if that was on her left or right hand?"

"Let me think about it. She struck the match with her right hand and cupped my cigarette with her left hand, so—yeah, it was on her right hand."

"Thanks, Frank. That is some good information."

Frank started to reach into his vest pocket. "In fact, she handed me the book of matches when she walked off with the others. Looks like it's from one of those girlie joints, if you know what I mean."

"Yeah, Frank, I do. Can I see the matches?"

"Sure."

It was a half-used book of matches from Jo's Hideaway. Sounded like a girlie place to me too. "Do you mind if I take these, Frank?"

"Nah, go ahead, I don't have any more smokes anyway."

"So, Frank, did the three of them leave after talking with you?"

"They walked away from me and I could hardly hear what they were saying. I just remember the floozy gal arguing with them, saying no way she was going with them. Then she ended up walking away from them."

"Do you know what they were arguing over?"

"Nope! ... Oh, hey, I remember something ... when the floozy was walking away from the other two, the guy called out to her and used the name of Candi."

"Candi? Thanks. Then the other two stayed around for a while on the pier after Candi left?"

"Right after she walked away, the other two got on the boat. It was pretty quiet and I think I fell back asleep then."

"So you didn't hear anything—no arguing or fighting on the yacht after they boarded?"

"No. Like I said, I fell back asleep and it wasn't until the motor started up and the boat went out to sea that I woke up again."

"And do you recall about how much time passed between the time they first approached you on the pier and when the boat went back out to sea?"

"Maybe an hour. All three of them seemed a little drunk and didn't seem real sure of what they were doing." Frank took another swig from his wine bottle—which was already nearly empty.

I looked over at Brad and asked him if he had any questions for Frank, but he appeared to be pleased with all the information we had already gleaned. He handed me the second bottle of wine for Frank.

"Thanks, Frank. You've been very helpful and we might be stopping by again some time to say hello." I handed him the second bottle of wine and his eyes lit up again.

"Sure, guys. Come by any time. You know where you can find me."

As Brad and I walked back to the car, we were both trying to maintain our composure. We were practically giddy inside from what we'd just learned.

Finally, Brad couldn't hold back any longer. "That … was … AWESOME! Hon, you were amazing back there."

"Thanks, Brad, but it doesn't always have such a successful outcome. At any rate, now you have a better idea of what it is that I do when I'm so consumed by an intriguing case such as this."

"Awesome! That is all I can say. The way you kept pulling Frank in and getting him to open up to you. I am totally impressed!"

"Thanks, Babe."

As we exited the harbor parking lot, my mind was racing with all the details I had just learned. I was anxious to get it all down on paper. "You know I'm going to rely on you, Brad, to double check my memory with all this stuff."

With excitement in his voice, he responded, "I'm sure between the two of us when we get back home we can recount everything."

"I know one thing for sure ... you and I will be making a little trip soon to Jo's Hideaway. Are you up for a little girly peep show Brad?"

"Oh, gawd. The things I do for you, Tony."

12

Jo's Hideaway

Once back at the condo, I googled Jo's Hideaway and learned that it was located in an industrial area of San Diego in the south part of town, actually not all that far from the Elite Limo garage I'd visited earlier.

Brad and I talked it over and decided to check out Jo's on Wednesday evening. This would give me some time to organize my thoughts. I wanted to check with Chief Tallerico too, and see if he had anything new for me, and what he'd decided on to do about arresting Rudy.

Talking with the Chief the next afternoon, he confirmed that he had questioned Rudy and agreed with my findings. Rudy apparently was not the murderer, and his alibi checked out. There was nothing new from the police investigation end of things, at least nothing that the Chief was willing to share. And I had no intention of sharing with him the new lead that I had. This was my case and I was hot on it.

Wednesday evening arrived before we knew it. I was

excited about the prospect of what we might learn from this excursion and a bit uneasy at the thought of going to a stripper bar. ... Not that I'd never been in a stripper bar, but I admit I don't recall doing so when the strippers on stage were women! Brad seemed to be excited about going along with me again, but I don't think he was all that thrilled with going to a strip bar either and playing it up like he was a straight man. I told him it's all just part of the job and going undercover.

Pulling up to the front of Jo's Hideaway, we noticed that the windows were all blacked out and the building almost appeared to be abandoned. We saw a small business sign on the front door and a couple of beer signs in the transom windows. The asphalt parking lot, laden with potholes, had maybe a half dozen cars parked. It was shortly after nine o'clock on a weeknight, so I didn't expect a large crowd.

Once again, I was happy to have Brad with me, and it was time for the two of us to "butch" it up upon entering this obviously redneck establishment.

As we approached the front door, I turned to Brad with a sigh, "We're not in Kansas anymore, Toto."

The front door creaked as I pushed it open and we entered the dark abyss. Dim light emanated from the wine bottle candles on each table and from lighted beer signs behind the bar. As our eyes adjusted, I realized everyone, all six customers, had turned to see who had just arrived. New patrons apparently served to pique their curiosity—so much for trying not to be noticed!

We found a table not far from the large U-shaped bar at the center of the back wall and then realized we were seated next to a stage. I could only imagine what might take place on that stage—and when I focused on the chrome pole center stage, my suspicions were confirmed. I hoped this was not a performance night.

While we waited for the cocktail waitress to come over and take our order, suddenly a spotlight flooded the stage and shown on the two of us as well. The strains of "Witchy Woman" began to fill the room and a young woman with purple-streaked hair and matching pasties appeared on stage and began foreplay with the pole right in front of us. This was going to be more of a challenging mission than I expected.

It wasn't long before a perky gal with boobs overflowing her tube top showed up to take our order. "Hey, Doll Face. What can I get you boys?"

I tried not to look as she leaned over to wipe off our table and make sure we had a clear shot of her silicone boobs that she was obviously quite proud of. Brad seemed more uncomfortable with the display than I was, and appeared to be blushing—although it was hard to tell for sure in the candlelight.

Then as her right hand with a dish rag circled the table, I focused on a rose tattoo on the back of her hand.

This was the gal ... this was Candi!

I never expected things would happen this quickly once we got inside and I was not sure what to do next.

"Ahh, yeah, sure ... I'll have a Corona with lime," I managed to stutter.

Looking at Brad, she asked, "And for you, darlin'?"

I was sure that Brad had not noticed the tattoo. He was probably trying too hard not to focus on the boobs. "I'll have a vodka tonic, thanks."

After she walked away I clued Brad into the identity of the waitress and the rose tattoo.

"Well, that was easy," Brad commented.

I was glad the bar was not too busy as I could likely get some time to talk with Candi and have her undivided attention.

"Here you go, boys. Did you want to run a tab on that?"

"Sure!" I spoke up. "And is your name Candi, by chance?"

"It sure is, Sugar. Do we have a mutual friend?"

I had my business card in my hand and I slid it across the table to her. "Not exactly, Candi." I introduced myself to her as a Private Investigator and Brad as my associate. Her demeanor changed immediately.

"Well, it's nice to meet you both but I'm a little busy now."

"What time do you go on a break? I'd like to talk with you briefly if you don't mind."

"Well, Honey, I just don't know. Besides, I don't think I can help you with anything."

"I'm sure you can, Candi. I think you were on a late night tryst with a couple about two weeks ago on a Saturday night that took you to the Large Ships pier. Does that sound familiar?"

"I'm not sure—I don't recall. ... Look, I need to get back to work here."

"Well, tell me when you go on break so we can talk more."

"I said I really don't have anything to say to you."

"Well, if you don't want to talk to me, you can talk to the police when I turn you in and they haul your ass down to the station for questioning as an accessory to murder."

"What the hell are you talking about ... murder?"

"Just tell me when and where we can talk, Miss Candi."

"Okay. I have a thirty-minute dinner break at 10:45. I can talk with you then, but not out here on the floor. You can meet me out back. I'll take my break there and we can talk. Now I gotta go."

"Thanks. See you at 10:45 out back."

For the next hour Candi treated us as if we were invisible. She would never make eye contact with us and never came near our table to ask if we wanted another round of drinks. I was beginning to think she wasn't going to show up at our planned location behind the bar.

At 10:45 Candi seemed to have already made herself scarce on the floor. I told Brad I'd meet him out in front of the bar after paying the bartender for our tab. I left a few bucks tip on the table for Candi even though her service clearly didn't warrant a gratuity.

I found Brad just outside the front door. "Well, shall we walk around back and see if Candi keeps her word and shows up to talk with us?"

"Sure, Tony. I think this side is the best way to get to the back door." We walked off around the right side of the building adjacent to the parking lot.

There she was. Candi was already smoking the first of many cigarettes when we walked up. "So what's all this garbage about me being mixed up with some murder investigation? I have no idea what you're talking about."

"Let me explain. On the night of Saturday, July 13, a Bastille Day yacht party took place at sea. The yacht docked at the pier after midnight, and sometime after docking, a young man was murdered aboard the yacht. I have reason to believe you may have had contact with the couple I suspect committed the murder. Does any of this sound familiar to you, Candi?"

Her eyes got wide but she remained quiet. I could tell she knew something but was hesitant to talk.

The long pause of silence was uncomfortable. "Fine, Candi. If you don't want to talk with me, I'm sure the police would be more than happy to haul you in for interrogation. I'm not about to waste my time with you."

I started to walk off. . . . "No, wait! . . . Geeze, I don't know how I could have gotten myself into this mess.

... Yeah, I do know or should I say I met the man and woman you're talking about."

"Okay, then. Why don't you tell us about it, from the beginning? How did you meet them?"

"Geeze. I was working that Saturday night. As with most weekends, it was a busy night and the crowd was pretty wild. Made a lot of tip money that night too. There was this one couple that I enjoyed joking around with all night and they were slammin' them down pretty good and tipping me good too."

"Do you recall their names?" I reached for my notepad and Cross pen.

"Yeah, sure I do. I ended up partying with them after the bar closed down. The guy was Jack and his old lady was Lisa. They were crazy fun but pretty wild, it seemed to me." This statement coming from Candi made me wonder just how off the wall they could have been.

"So, what happened after you got off work and the bar closed down?"

"Well, we locked the doors and had one more drink after closing. Even though the ABC boys don't approve of that, we do it all the time. When they got ready to leave, they wanted me to go with them and said they were going to go have some more fun. After working a shift like that, I was ready to party too. You ever work in the bar business?"

"I worked as a waiter and served drinks. I know

exactly what you mean when you've had a busy night, and you're still hyped up after you get off work." I related to her. ". . . So what did you do? Did you go with them?"

"Well, they seemed like good people and they had tipped me well all night and so I decided to go with them for a while. I wanted to take my own car but they said it would be better if we rode together. They insisted I climb into their Caddy with them."

"So at that late hour, where did you go?"

"Well, he drove off like he was on a mission and knew exactly where he was going. I was in the back seat and not paying too much attention but then the next thing I knew we were at the pier. When I asked him what the hell we were doing there, he just said we were going to party, and ordered me to get out."

"Was he mad at this time or did his disposition seem to change from the party animal in the bar?"

"Not really. He just kept saying he was going to take me on a joy ride and party and have a good time. . . . So we walked down the pier to a large boat that was docked and he said 'there she is . . . that's my boat.' Of course I didn't believe him."

"So what was Lisa doing all this time? Did she say much?"

"She was pretty quiet and seemed to go along with everything that Jack said. She was sort of mousey, if you know the type."

"So was this when you met the old homeless man on the pier?"

"Geeze, how do you know about that?"

"As I said, Candi, I'm a Private Investigator—it's my job."

"Well, you must be pretty damn good at it. Anyway, yeah, we struck up a conversation with this old homeless dude sleeping on the pier. In fact, I think I gave him a cigarette ... speaking of which, excuse me." Candi reached for another cigarette herself and puffed a cloud of smoke nearly into my face after getting it lit.

"So what happened from that point, Candi?"

"Well, this guy Jack said he actually didn't own the boat but had a key to it. He said something about having worked for the owner who he claimed was an asshole and had fired him because he wasn't gay and he was going to just take the boat out and have some fun with it. He said the owner owed that to him. He was insistent about going and wanted me to come with them. Lisa seemed afraid of him at that point, and let me know she wanted me to come too because I think she was getting worried about what he might do."

"Like what ... did he seem violent or mean at this point?"

"He seemed to be getting more agitated the more we argued, and then finally I told him there was no way I was going aboard that boat and I walked off. I told him I'd take a cab back to my car and to go and have his fun. ... I didn't stop to think how late it was and that it might be difficult getting a cab. ... There were some characters out and about at that time of the night, but I pack heat in my purse and I'm not afraid to use it if I need to. I wasn't too worried. Lucky for me there was a cruise ship docked and some of the passengers were just getting back from a night out on the town, so I caught their cab back to my car."

"And when you walked away, you left the two of them on the pier?"

"Yes, but I have no doubt they took that boat out later from the way Jack was talking."

"Well, someone took that boat out later and murdered a young man who was on board and then tried to cover up the murder. . . . Do you know Jack or Lisa's last names?"

"No, I've seen them in the bar before, but that was the first time I'd spent any time with them . . . Jack is a regular here."

"Really? So he's been in during the last week or so?" I expected, if he had committed this murder, he would be lying low and not be out in public for a while.

"Oh, yeah! He comes in for Ladies Night on Thursdays, like clockwork. Drinks are half price for the ladies. Then he usually comes in on Saturdays too."

"So, Candi, you think he'll be in tomorrow night then?"

"I'd almost stake my life on it. Always sits at the same spot at the bar too."

"We want to come back tomorrow and get a look at this guy. Do you think there's any way we can find out his last name?"

"Well, if he was new, I could card him, but he's a

regular. He would get suspicious of that, I'm sure."

"Does Lisa come in with him?"

"Nah. She'll show up later and join him but he's usually here early. You can't miss Lisa. She's short, about five feet with bleached blond hair in a pixie cut. Looks like a little munchkin."

"Thanks. This has all been very helpful. We'll plan to come back tomorrow night and see what we can find out about these two."

"You know, I gotta get back to work but I just thought of something. Jack always likes to run a tab. Tomorrow night I could feed him a line that the new management wants us to get a credit card or driver's license on all tabs until they're paid up. How does that sound?"

"Great! ... And I appreciate you doing that as long as you don't get in trouble with the management."

"No problem. I sleep with the owner, so I sort of am the management." She smiled and gave a shrug of her shoulder.

"Well, thanks Candi. We'll see you tomorrow night."

"Great! See you then."

Driving home, Brad was sounding a little concerned that things were starting to get too dangerous, being so close to finding the murderer. "Tony, you think maybe now you should turn all this information over to the police and let them investigate further?"

"No way! I'm hot on solving this thing now and I want to get the credit for it. But you don't have to come tomorrow if this is getting too intense for you. I know you're not used to this kind of thing."

"There's no way I'm letting you come out here alone—that's for sure."

"Great. It's a date for Ladies Night at Jo's Hideaway."

I considered what Brad had said and wondered if I should let Chief Tallerico know all that I'd recently learned, but I knew he would take over and ask me to step aside. I wasn't ready for that quite yet. Besides not having a lot of faith in the Chief's conclusions so far, I was afraid he might botch the entire investigation and Gus's murderer just might get away.

I decided I would let my boss, Vinnie, know where I was with this investigation as I felt sure he was wondering why I had been so unavailable lately. I was feeling guilty that I had not been better at keeping in touch with the office. I planned to call in, first thing in the morning.

13

Undercover

It was just after ten o'clock Thursday evening when Brad and I entered Jo's Hideaway and took a seat at the same table we'd sat at the night before.

"Hey, Boys, how y'all doing tonight? . . . What can I get you?"

"Hey, Candi . . . busy night tonight? I'll have a Corona with lime."

"And I'll have a vodka tonic. Thanks, Candi," Brad responded.

While we waited for our drinks, our eyes adjusted somewhat to the darkness. We looked around and easily spotted Jack seated at the bar. The tousled red hair was like a beacon in the illumination of the neon signs.

"Here you go, fellas. I brought you the bill too, but you just let me know if you want another one."

"Okay, thanks." I looked down at the tray with the bill and noticed a driver's license. With a wink, Candi turned and walked away.

There it was. Jack's driver's license. This was all the information I needed to track down Jack and have the police bring him in for questioning. Candi had really come through for us.

I took the driver's license into the men's room and photographed it with my iPhone. When Candi walked by our table, I handed her the tray with our money and returned the license to her along with a sizeable tip.

"Thanks, Candi."

Having successfully completed this part of our mission it was time for part two. Brad knew the plan so he quickly finished up his drink and we left the bar.

Once back at my car in the parking lot, we sat there in the dark, trying not to be noticed, and waited for Lisa to show—and hoping that it wouldn't be long. It was nearly 10:45 and I had the impression she usually joined Jack at eleven or so.

Sure enough, about ten minutes later a car drove up and we focused on a blond woman matching the description that Candi had given us. After she entered the bar, I shined my headlights on her license plate and Brad wrote down the number. I hoped this car was registered in her name and we'd have all the information we needed on her as well.

Brad was nervous about all of this. "Okay. Let's get the hell outta here."

"One more thing, Brad. I'll be right back. I want to

go back inside and make sure that this gal is seated with Jack so we're sure this is Lisa."

"Are you crazy? Let's just go ... Tony ... please?"

"Just let me do this and then we're done. I'll be right back."

I left the car and went back into the bar. I noticed Jack was no longer seated where he'd been when we'd left, and was now sitting at a table with the blond woman we'd observed in the parking lot. My expectations were confirmed. They were a couple ... we had them!

So as not to seem too conspicuous, I decided to use the men's room before leaving. Walking into the bar and turning around to leave would look a bit out of the ordinary and might draw too much attention. Besides ... I had to pee. The men's room was down a short hallway of knotty pine paneling toward the back of the bar—dark and very near the back exit. Candi didn't seem to notice my return and so I easily slipped unnoticed into the men's room. That was the last thing I remembered.

When I started coming to, I was in the back seat of a car with a hood over my head and my hands bound behind my back. I realized that I must have been knocked unconscious in the men's room, and hustled out the back door and into a waiting car. My head hurt like crazy, but I remained still and tried to listen to what was being said to get a clue as to what was happening and where we were headed.

From what I could tell, there were three other men in the vehicle with me. The two in the front seat spoke with a Brooklyn accent that sounded oddly familiar to me. The one sitting next to me in the back spoke clearly with no accent.

The men were talking about their plans to dispose of me on their next "run," whatever that meant. The word dispose did not sound good to me, however.

We drove for what seemed to be only a very short distance unless I'd been unconscious longer than I realized. When we stopped, I was pretty sure we were some place not far from Jo's Hideaway.

∽

Brad was growing very concerned that I hadn't returned to the car where he was waiting. He went back into Jo's again to see if I was still inside or if Candi knew anything. Candi hadn't noticed me come back into the bar and told Brad she hadn't seen me. He noticed that Jack and Lisa were still there, very casually laughing and being a little amorous with one another. If he'd had any suspicion about them harming me, seeing them nonchalantly enjoying the evening changed all that. He realized there was apparently someone else who was interested in my investigation.

Brad decided to check the men's room, fearful of what

he could possibly find there ... such as my dead body. He was relieved to find the men's room empty. As he turned to leave and reached to open the door, he noticed the glittering of a gold pen on the floor, a gold Cross pen ... my gold Cross pen. In the scuffle of rendering me unconscious, my pen had been dislodged from my shirt pocket and left behind. Brad knew I'd never leave my favorite pen anywhere. He panicked as he realized there was foul play involved and that I was gone, probably abducted, and hopefully nothing worse.

Brad's set of keys included the key to my Honda, so he drove directly to the police station. He was told that, since there was no obvious sign of foul play, they couldn't take a report for a missing person until 24 hours had passed. Brad was devastated by this news and decided to be in Chief Tallerico's office when he showed up first thing in the morning. He was going to tell the Chief everything and turn over the information we'd gathered on Jack and Lisa and the vagrant and all of it. Fortunately, when I'd gone back into the restroom at the bar, I'd left my cell phone in the car. The photograph of Jack's driver's license and all the information on Jack was right there on my phone.

My three captors got out and talked outside the car for a while. I couldn't make out what they were saying but it sounded like there were more than just the three men now. The backseat car door was opened, and they realized I was conscious when I inadvertently groaned from my splitting headache. I was pulled out and forced to walk with the hood still on my head.

As we walked over old crumbling asphalt, I realized the man holding me firm on my right side walked with a limp. Why was this familiar to me? I tried to look down from under the hood to catch a glimpse of him, but the flap of material around my neck kept getting in the way. I kept moving my head to see if I could get a glimpse. It was dark but there was street lighting that illuminated our path more so at times than others. It reminded me a lot of the area around the pier with the missing and broken lights.

I continued moving my head from side to side and up and down. Then at last, I saw his feet—and his built-up shoe. My heart was nearly beating out my chest as I recognized the man who now held me captive. It was Bruno, the security guard I'd interviewed early on in my investigation ... the one I'd ruled out since he'd had so little contact with the two party crashers attempting to come aboard the yacht.

14

Hostage

I heard a door slide open. It sounded like a warehouse door on rollers and I could smell the stench of oil and grease. I was pretty sure I was in an old shop building, possibly in the industrial area near the pier. There was a familiar ocean fish smell that I detected as well that further supported my suspicion that we were at or near the pier. I was forced into what seemed like a small office room and shoved to the floor and told to keep my mouth shut. I could hear the door lock as the men exited, leaving me alone . . . hands still bound and hood still on.

As I sat there on the floor in the darkness, I could hear the men arguing outside in the main warehouse building. The volume of the conversation seemed to fluctuate depending on how much disagreement between the men there was. I heard one of the guys say something about taking me out right now and leaving me for shark bait. One of the other men said it was too risky and that they should wait and take me with them down to Mexico on Sunday to dispose of the body. Either way, my fate appeared to be dismal at best. I needed to get the hell out of there . . . alive.

❧

Brad spent the night worried and pacing the floor. At the first light of day Friday morning, he headed down to the police station to wait for Chief Tallerico to come in to his office. He confirmed with the receptionist that the Chief was on his way in and was expecting to meet with me for some very important information.

Brad referenced my name to get the Chief's attention. Not having met the Chief before, he wondered how he might be received once he identified himself as Tony's other half.

After hearing Brad's story, the Chief was very concerned that foul play had indeed entered into this investigation and that I might be in danger . . . serious danger. He had his men begin a missing person's investigation immediately. He also issued an arrest order for Jack and Lisa. The Chief said it seemed quite obvious to him, from what Brad and I had uncovered, that this couple had something to do with the murder. He was convinced that they most likely had killed Gus themselves, but couldn't figure how they were involved in my being missing.

Brad watched from the observation room as the police questioned first Jack and then Lisa separately. Both of them denied having been anywhere near the pier the night of the Bastille Day party but their stories didn't match. When the police told them they had eye witnesses who could put them on the pier at the time the party guests were arriving, plus a report from a security guard that showed they were at that location, they changed their stories. Both of them admitted to being there early in the evening but said they'd left and hadn't returned. Something was just not right with these two and they were hiding something.

Chief Tallerico called Brad into his office. "Well, Brad, I wish I had some good news for you about Tony but my men are still on it. ... I do want to give you an update on the two suspects. It appears obvious to me that these two had something to do with the death of Gus. But I'm not sure what that is yet because the fingerprints on the murder object don't match either Jack's or Lisa's."

"Damn it. I'd have sworn they did it." Brad was shaking his head in disbelief.

"Well, I'm not saying they didn't but it's looking like there might be others involved."

"I just want Tony back, unharmed."

"We're working on that. He's a good man. We'll find him and get him home."

"Thanks, Chief."

❧

Sitting on the cold concrete floor, I could see daylight filtering into the room from somewhere. It had been quiet outside the locked door for what seemed to be several hours. I knew I had to try and break out of there if I wanted to stay alive. With my hands still tied behind my back, I began to slide around the filthy floor, looking for some sharp object that might be able to cut my ropes.

There were many iron objects within my reach but all seemed to be very rounded or blunt edged, not suitable for sawing through my bindings. I located some fishnet hanging on the wall and began to rub my head against it with hopes of removing the fabric hood covering my head. I could shift the hood a bit, but couldn't get it off. I kept trying, and after about a dozen attempts, I was able to get the hood over my eyes to my forehead and then fling it off me. I could now see where I was and it was not good.

There were no windows and from the looks of things this was a marine warehouse. I noticed anchors and ropes and miscellaneous objects that further indicated to me we might be near the pier. Then I spotted something that might be my salvation, a large ship's propeller. It was old and rusty but the blades were finely honed from many hours of cutting through the water. I backed up to it and began sawing my ropes. I felt the blade knick my wrist and I could tell this was going to take a while, but it appeared to be working. I was just hoping to not get caught trying to escape.

The rope frayed finally and broke, setting my hands free. Now what was I going to do? I hadn't thought that far ahead yet. I heard voices outside my door and maneuvering of the lock. I quickly pulled the hood back over my head and sat down on the floor with my hands behind my back, hoping they would think I was still bound. . . . It worked.

The men began to argue again and they finally decided to deal with me later since they couldn't come to an agreement. I heard Bruno say to lock the door and leave me alone. It appeared Bruno was the ringleader, the one giving the orders. Once the door was locked I pulled off the hood and began to survey the situation and see if there was any possible way of escaping this dungeon.

I saw no crawl space, but I noticed a ceiling wind turbine for air circulation. I could see daylight as the turbine turned ever so slowly and realized this was the light source I'd noticed. The hole in the ceiling was about ten feet up, and about 24 inches square, but this seemed like the only way out. Whatever I did, I had to be quiet and fast to avoid being caught.

I noticed a rickety old ladder, barely distinguishable under a pile of old tools and equipment. I managed to quietly retrieve it and hoped it would get me close to the hole in the ceiling. I realized it was not going to be tall enough to reach the turbine, but it was a start. There was a work bench that would give me about three extra feet if I could move it into place under the turbine without attracting attention. I surprised myself with my strength and composure. I moved the table into position, barely making a sound, and quickly set the ladder on top. It was perfect. I was fearful that the eroded rungs of the ladder wouldn't hold my weight, but I had to give it a try. This was my only option.

I heard each rung creak and crack as it seemed to struggle to hold up under my weight. Once at the top, I was not sure how I would manage to remove the turbine and clear an opening to pull myself through. The metal of the turbine was fastened into the wooden frame, but it seemed as old and rotted as the ladder. I grasped the metal turbine and felt it move. I hoped this was going to be easier than I thought, as long as I didn't make too much noise.

The turbine popped out with a loud snap of tin, exposing a clear crawl space to the roof of the warehouse. I froze, standing there at the top of my construction pyramid, hoping no one had heard. I could still hear the loud voices of the men arguing and apparently that had been enough to cover whatever noise I had made. I laid the metal frame carefully on the roof, leaving a clear passage for my escape. I knew I'd have to call upon my upper body strength to somehow pull myself up through the opening and out onto the roof. I thought of my high school days when I'd been named number one in my class for pull-ups in gym class, but of course that was many years ago. The threat of death was quite a motivator, and this was my only hope.

With a couple of deep breaths, I pulled myself up and was able to hook my elbow over the edge and then get my knee up onto the roof and pull myself through. I was now on the roof, free from the room but still in considerable danger from my captors. If they should catch me trying to escape, they would surely kill me.

The voices were coming from the front of the building, and I slowly snaked myself to the outside edge to peek over the side in hopes of getting a glimpse of these men so I could identify them later. They were arguing still, as they seemed to do most of the time, and I counted five of them standing around. I hoped that no one was inside the building and that the chances of my being heard on the roof were diminished. It flashed through my mind that their inability to get along was providing me the cover I needed to escape.

I recognized Bruno among the five men and got a good look at the other four. I knew I needed to get out of there and quickly. It looked to be about a ten-foot drop from the roof to safety, so I scanned the area looking for a discarded piece of rope or anything that could help me down. I quietly crawled to the back of the building, farthest away from the men, and noticed a downspout. This seemed like the only possible way to get down.

I grabbed hold of the gutter and dropped my body over, grasping tightly to the downspout. It appeared to be rather flimsy and weak but held my weight . . . at least briefly. I slid down about halfway before the downspout broke away from the fasteners on the wall and I fell hard to the ground and dry grass below me. The noise created from my fall seemed to me like a sonic boom, but maybe it was not all that loud and had gone unnoticed by the men at the front of the building.

There I sat in the grass, like a scared rabbit, not knowing what to do next. My heart was pounding with fear that any minute someone would come rushing around the side of the building. . . . I was now free, but what next? Where could I go? How could I get out of there unnoticed?

At the police station, some progress had been made and there'd been a breakthrough in the investigation. Lisa had cracked under the pressure and admitted that she and Jack had taken the yacht out that night. She said they'd seen a dead body on the yacht when they boarded and she had begged Jack to leave. But he'd been insistent on taking the boat out for a joy ride and she said she couldn't change his mind.

"This is good news, Brad," said the Chief, "but I'm sorry we still don't have any news on who killed Gus."

"And . . . we still don't know where Tony is!"

"We're doing all we can to find him, but solving the murder might lead us to him," said the Chief, as he reached out and put his hand on Brad's shoulder.

"Lisa insists it was just the two of them that night," he continued. Apparently someone else had taken over the yacht before they'd even gotten there—someone who might have had a reason to kill Gus. Or possibly he was just an innocent victim, left lying naked on the floor—an innocent victim who happened to be in the wrong place at the wrong time."

꩜

From the back of the warehouse I could see fishermen on a small pier about a football field away. I knew if I took off running I'd surely be noticed because the area between me and the pier was pretty wide open. Using the warehouse for cover, I climbed over a small rock wall down onto the bank along the water's edge, onto the riprap that lined the shore. I scrambled my way over the rocks, staying below the parking lot surface and keeping out of sight of Bruno and the others.

Now a safe distance away, I ran to find someone on the pier with a cell phone to call Chief Tallerico. With luck, these thugs wouldn't even realize I was missing until the police got there.

"Hello, this is Tallerico." The Chief sounded stressed.

"Chief, this is Tony."

"Tony! Where in the hell are you? We've been looking for you. Are you all right? Your friend Brad is here, and is worried sick."

"Listen, Chief, I was held hostage but I'm free now. Can you send your men out to arrest these guys? They don't know yet that I've escaped."

"Sure, Tony. Where are you?"

"I'm at the south end of the Large Ships pier, near the dry dock area. The kidnappers, five of them, are in an old marine warehouse there, not far from the fishing pier. They're driving a black Lincoln Navigator and a burgundy Mercury Marquis."

"Great. I'll send my men out right away. Where are *you* now?"

"I'm on the fishing pier using someone's cell phone here. Hurry because I know once these guys realize I'm gone, they'll be out of here."

"No problem. We're on our way right now."

Brad was in Chief Tallerico's office at the time of my call and was smiling ear to ear at learning I was alive.

"Let's go, Brad. Let's go pick up your boy, Tony."

"Thanks, Chief."

Within about ten minutes of my call, I observed three police cars racing up and surrounding the warehouse, followed by two more police cars. I could hear gunshots and noticed a lot of scrambling of men and vehicles. An ambulance arrived and I could see one man being loaded in the back while four others were handcuffed and secured in the back of police cars.

Then I saw a police car headed toward me on the pier and realized it was Chief Tallerico—and Brad was riding shotgun with him. I've never been so happy to see his face. Brad bounded from the vehicle and ran to me. We embraced and I never wanted to let him go. It was such a relief to be alive.

Holding me away, Brad said, "Let me look at you … God, you look like hell. Are you all right?" We chuckled as I took a quick inventory and realized my hands were scratched, my butt and ankle hurt, my pants were torn, I was filthy from crawling along the roof and the riprap, and the bump on my head still throbbed. But I was alive and, for the most part, okay.

The investigation was now in the hands of the police, but I was pretty sure I now knew who the murderer was, just not sure of the motive, or if there was one.

Chief Tallerico looked at me. "C'mon, Tony, I'm taking you and Brad home." It occurred to me at that point that the "Mr. Felice" formality had given way to the friendlier use of "Tony." And I didn't mind a bit.

"Thanks, Chief. There's nothing I'd like more."

15

Mystery Solved

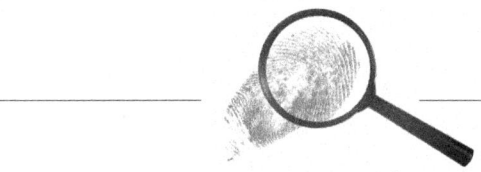

It was so nice to be home, and such a relief having the investigation pretty well wrapped up. I was still curious to find out the sequence of events that had lead up to Gustavo's death, but that would all come in time.

Finally reunited with my iPhone, I realized I had several new messages. They were all from my boss who was wondering if I had been abducted by aliens. That was not far from the truth. In my obsession with this case, I'd forgotten to check in with work as I usually did a few times a week. Vinnie was getting a little worried.

"Tony, where are you? Jenn said you haven't been in the office and haven't called in. I hope everything is all right with you. Give me a call and let me know what's happening. . . . Okay. Hope to hear from you soon."

I hated to leave Brad, but I thought it would be best if I stopped by the office. I needed to explain the details of the last few days of my investigation, leading up to my captivity and the eventual arrest of Jack and Lisa and

Bruno and his band of men. I still wasn't sure how Bruno and his boys fit into this scenario but it was obvious they were guilty of something.

After my quick stop at the office, I was looking forward to a nice quiet evening at home, cuddled in the arms of my man and with no thoughts of the investigation running through my head. Brad, on the other hand, entertained different thoughts.

"I am so proud of you, Hon," Brad gloated with a smile on his face much like that of the Cheshire Cat.

"Thanks, Brad. It's been a rough couple of weeks but I'm glad this whole thing is over and we've found Gus's murderer."

"Well, tonight I think we should celebrate, just the two of us. . . . I'm taking you to dinner for Chinese."

"Yum, how can I resist . . . my favorite. Wang's, North Park?"

"Of course. What else is there?"

"Thanks, Babe, you always seem to know what I need." I couldn't tell him I would just as soon stay home for the evening. But I do enjoy the relaxing atmosphere at Wang's and I could surely use that.

We had a very nice evening with some great conversation—just us, reconnecting. That, of course, meant having our cell phones off so we wouldn't be interrupted and could enjoy each other's company. When we got home late that night, I had a message from Chief Tallerico.

"Tony, this is Tallerico. ... Can you stop by my office tomorrow? I want to go over the case with you and let you know what we discovered from our interrogation of the suspects that we arrested. I'm sure you'll find it all very interesting since you worked so closely ... actually solved the case for us. Can you come by after two? I'll be expecting you. Thanks."

❧

As I walked up the front steps to the police station, I had butterflies in my stomach in anticipation of learning the full details of the murder. I had so many unanswered questions in my head. I was looking forward to having all that cleared up.

"Good afternoon, Mr. Felice. Chief Tallerico is expecting you. I'll let him know you're here."

"Thanks!"

Chief Tallerico came out to greet me and we walked back into his office. I could feel the change in his attitude toward me from the first day I walked into his office and introduced myself.

"I wanted to thank you, Tony, for your work on this case. Excellent job investigating."

"Thanks, Chief. It means a lot to me to hear you say that."

"So let me tell you what we learned, now that we've been able to put all the pieces of the puzzle together. It appears that although Jack and Lisa are both in big trouble, they are not the murderers. That night of the party, Jack and Lisa were drunk. He took Lisa over to the yacht and was telling everyone that he had a right to be there at the party. After they were escorted off the pier, he became more angered from the embarrassment, and he continued to get drunker as the night went on. Jack decided he was going to steal the yacht and take it for a joy ride, with intentions of bringing it back after having some fun.

"Turns out, Jack was Robert de Saint Cyr's former chef for several years before he was let go and Gus was hired to take his place. Jack resented that, and felt Gus received preferential treatment, being a good-looking young gay man and Jack being straight.

"So that night when they boarded the yacht, and went down below, they found Gus, lying at the foot of the stairs in a pool of his own blood. Jack stepped over Gus's naked body, and continued with his plans for a joy ride. Lisa wanted to leave, but Jack was insistent on his mission and, being drunk, persisted in taking the yacht out for a spin.

"Once out at sea, Jack realized what he'd done and that he could be considered the prime suspect in this boy's death. But the liquor had got the best of him, and instead of trying at this point to make things right, Jack continued with his bad judgment by deciding to sink the evidence, including Gus's body. He placed a small fuel can he found on board near the propane heater, figuring that the fumes would eventually explode into flames and the burning yacht would sink. Then he and Lisa jumped in the small rescue motor boat secured to the yacht and headed back to shore.

"What Jack didn't count on was that the heater's propane canister was nearly empty and ran out of fuel before the point of combustion. Jack and Lisa did manage to make it to shore in the small motor boat and they thought they'd escaped getting caught and had covered their tracks."

I was still a little puzzled. "So that still leaves the question of who killed Gus and why."

"I'm getting to that." The Chief let out a big sigh as he started with the second part of his story.

"Good."

"So, turns out we have another crime solved here. It appears that Bruno and his boys have been stealing boats to run drugs up the coast from Ensenada for quite some time and making a pretty good living from it. Bruno's job as a security guard was just a cover-up and not his primary source of income, by a long shot.

"Bruno worked the Bastille Day party but had plans for the 'GODY-GO' later that night. He and his boys planned to steal the yacht and make a drug run, bringing back more than 200 pounds of pure cocaine into the states.

"What Bruno didn't plan on was finding Gus sleeping on board. It was dark when he and his thugs started down the stairs of the yacht to the promenade deck, and Gus was startled from his sleep. Naked, he decided to investigate what all the commotion was about and that was his mistake. In the dark he met Bruno on the stairway and they fought. Gus was thrown against the display case in the stairway, breaking the glass. Bruno grabbed for the first thing he could find in the dark— which happened to be Robert's Oscar for Best Directing of *Still Waters Run Deep*. He slugged Gus and his body tumbled down the stairs and slammed into the hard marble floor below. Bruno and his boys decided to scrap the drug run and got the hell out of there. By the time Jack and Lisa arrived, they were long gone.

"What Bruno failed to realize was that his fingerprints were all over the murder weapon and, once we had him in custody, there was no question as to who had killed Gus.

"With your help, Tony, we've been able to solve two crimes here, with the most serious, of course, being the murder. Jack and Lisa will not get off easy, however. They tried to destroy evidence and cover up a murder and will be charged with grand theft and malicious mischief. And despite the blow to Gus's head and his bleeding from glass cuts and the impact with the floor, it's possible he was still alive when Jack and Lisa found him. It's the opinion of the coroner that it would have taken quite a while for him to bleed to death on that marble floor. Jack and Lisa apparently never bothered to check for signs of life, just assumed he was dead. Had they done so, it's possible they could have saved his life. The district attorney will decide if any charges will be brought up in that regard.

"Bruno and his boys will be facing charges for running drugs and a string of prior thefts and destruction of property. Stealing large yachts for the purpose of drug running seemed to be a pattern over the years for them. This arrest clears up several cold cases we've had on the books. In addition to facing charges of murder, they face the charge of kidnapping you and holding you prisoner against your will. This should get them put away for quite a while, if not for life."

I sat there speechless for a moment. "Well, it all makes sense now . . . I guess."

"Yeah, as bizarre as it all seems, Gus was not a target, but merely an innocent young man in the wrong place," the Chief commented.

"This is a terrible loss," I said. "Gus was an excellent chef and a very reliable, dependable young man. I doubt seriously if Robert hired him merely because he was gay and handsome . . . and I don't think Robert is the type who would treat anyone unfairly."

The Chief continued, "It's quite obvious to me that

Jack had a drinking and psychological problem. He was clearly disgruntled from being fired and held a grudge, but I don't think he would ever contemplate murder. With Bruno, on the other hand, it's his way of life ... drugs and crime. He seems like one bad dude."

"You got that right, Chief." I said. "I want to thank you for your cooperation. I feel much better now that this is all behind me."

Chief Tallerico stood up and extended his hand to shake. "I'm sure you do. Thanks for all your help, Tony. I'm glad you're safe. ... You do realize you'll be called in to testify during the hearing?"

"Yes, of course."

"Again ... thank you, Tony ... you have my respect."

That last comment coming from the Chief really made me feel good. Our working relationship had matured and the respect was mutual. And—he had learned a bit more about the gay community that might serve him well in the future.

I had just pulled into our basement garage when my phone rang. The iPhone identified the caller as Robert de Saint Cyr.

"Hello, Robert. This is Tony."

"Hallo, Mr. Tony. I am just wanting to check back to you in hope you have news for me."

"I was just about to call you. I just came from the police station."

"And with some satisfaction, I am hopeful."

"Yes, very much so. The case is resolved and the bad guys are in jail. We'll have to get together soon so I can explain the details."

"No ... that is not my concern, Mr. Tony. It pleasures me to know that you have captured the murderer. It is no necessary that I should know any more."

"Okay."

"I owe you much thanks for you ability to take care of this for me and for Gus."

"Not a problem. I'm glad I could do this for Gus. I do wish he were still with us."

"Now I must reward you for your services. We had no talk about your pay when you agree to work for me."

"As I said, Robert, I'm more than happy to have offered my assistance, and glad to have this all behind us now."

"Oui, yes. It is much appreciated. I will post a check to you first thing in the morning. I hope you will find a hundred thousand dollars to be a fit compensation for you time."

I was silent for a moment, speechless. "Mr. de Saint Cyr, that is extremely generous of you. I don't know what to say. Thank you so much."

"It is my pleasure and much well deserved."

"Again, I'm glad I could help."

"Well, Mr. Tony, if our paths they don't meet in the near future, I look forward that you and Brad are my guests for my Bastille Day Party next year."

"Thank you, Robert. We look forward to it and to seeing you again."

One hundred thousand dollars! ... Along with the ten grand he'd already paid me as a retainer. I realized I had truly become one of San Diego's reputable Private Investigators and it felt good. It's Vinnie's policy that his percentage is taken only from the normal fee charged by the agency and that any bonus goes directly to the Investigator. In this case I would end up with roughly seventy five thousand dollars!

I got out of the car and headed up to the condo, a very big smile on my face. As I walked in the front door, Brad greeted me with a cosmo. I hugged him. "I love you so much, Babe. ... My life is so good! Everyone should want to be me."

Brad laughed. "Well, someone is sure full of himself."

"And ... with good reason," I said. "I'm taking you on a cruise. A cruise around the world if that is what you want, but you and I are going to celebrate."

"Well, I'm not going to argue with that." Brad had that look in his eye that I knew all too well. Instinctively, we both put down our drinks and fell into a passionate embrace, falling back onto the couch. We had some catching up to do. I was instantly aroused by the warm breath of his kiss and the feel of his body pressing against mine. We decided to continue this in the bedroom.

And so, over the next few months ... we began making plans for our Anniversary Cruise the following year. However, unbeknownst to me ... this would not turn out to be just any cruise. No ... this would be a cruise to remember.

"…Still waters run deep."

Acknowledgements

I would like to thank all those friends and family that supported me in the creation of this the second book in the Tony Felice mystery series. A special thank you to Sonya Cox for all the many hours spent editing my writing and making me look good.

And ... I'm sorry for having cursed my high school English teacher, Barbara Cannon. Thanks for teaching me some useful skills in life. Believe me, I appreciate you now.

And ... a special thank you to Palm Springs Koffi, south end for keeping my coffee cup full and putting up with me for all the hours that I spent writing this book at the coffee shop.

And ... thanks to the boy's at Triangle Inn for allowing me the freedom to be creative while being au natural by the resort pool. It's truly an inspiration to be able to be creative while free of textiles.

Did you enjoy reading about
Tony's adventure?

Want to read more?

Look for

NAKED DICK

on Amazon

Book 1 in the
Tony Felice mystery series.

www.TonyFeliceMystery.com

www.ingramcontent.com/pod-product-compliance
Lightning Source LLC
Chambersburg PA
CBHW060927180626
46817CB00004B/1433